WHISPERS
DOWN
THE LANE

SUMMERHILL SECRETS

Whispers Down the Lane
Secret in the Willows

WHISPERS DOWN THE LANE

Beverly Lewis

BETHANY HOUSE PUBLISHERS
MINNEAPOLIS, MINNESOTA 55438

Copyright © 1995
Beverly Lewis

Published by Bethany House Publishers
A Ministry of Bethany Fellowship, Inc.
11300 Hampshire Avenue South
Minneapolis, Minnesota 55438

Printed in the United States of America.

Library of Congress Cataloging-in-Publication Data

Lewis, Beverly
    Whispers down the lane / Beverly Lewis.
      p. cm. — (SummerHill secrets ; 1)
    Summary: After being beaten by her father, Lissa, an eighth grade classmate, comes to Merry's house in the middle of the night, and Merry asks God and the family of her Amish friend, Rachel, to help her protect Lissa.

    [1. Child abuse—Fiction. 2. Christian life—Fiction. 3. Amish—Fiction.]
I. Title. II. Series: Lewis, Beverly, 1949– SummerHill Secrets ; 1.
PZ7.L58464Wh 1994
[Fic]—dc20   94–49225
ISBN 1–55661–476–4   CIP
                                  AC

To

my aunt Ada Reba,

who held my little hand

long ago . . .

and whispered a prayer.

BEVERLY LEWIS is a best-selling author, speaker, and teacher. She has written more than twenty books for teens and children. Many of her articles and stories have appeared in the nation's top magazines.

A member of The National League of American Pen Women, the Society of Children's Book Writers and Illustrators, and Colorado Christian Communicators, Beverly lives with her husband, Dave, their three teenagers, and a crazy cockapoo named Cuddles, who snores to Mozart!

Happy is the house that shelters a friend.

—Ralph Waldo Emerson

ONE

A cry rang out in the stillness.

"Merry Hanson!"

I jerked into consciousness, tense and trembling. Sitting up, I peered out at my moonlit bedroom through sleep-filled eyes, listening. The gentle, steady purr of kittens filled the peaceful quiet. Their soft, warm bodies snuggled close on top of the comforter as I moved my feet.

Must be a dream. I leaned back onto my pillow, my body stiff from the rude awakening.

Then in the silence, I heard it again. A determined voice, quivering with desperation. "Merry, please wake up!"

Stumbling out of bed, I dashed to the window and looked out. Shadows played beneath the white light of a full November moon. One shadow stood out from the others and moved slowly toward the house.

I bumped my nose against the cold window as I stared down at a fragile-looking figure. Light from the moon had turned her wheat-colored hair almost white. I drew in a quick breath. *Lissa Vyner!*

Straining, I lifted the storm window and poked my head out into the frosty Pennsylvania night. Squinting down from the second story of our hundred-year-old farmhouse, I tried to brush the sleep away. My school friend was crouched near the old maple.

"Lissa, what are you doing out there?" I called to her in a hushed voice. Shivers danced up and down my arms.

She pulled her jacket against her body. "C-can I sp-spend the n-n-night?" she pleaded, tears in her voice.

"Meet me around back." I closed the window and scrambled for my robe and fleece-lined slippers. Shadrach and Meshach, my two golden-haired kittens, were curled up on it. "Sorry, little boys," I whispered, pulling it out from under their drowsy heads. "Where's Abednego?" *That ornery cat is always missing,* I thought.

Silently, I slipped down the hallway and past my older brother's room to the stairs. I didn't dare let Skip in on this thing with Lissa, especially since he was in charge while Mom and Dad were overseas on a mission trip.

I stopped in my tracks as I came within a few feet of the kitchen. Shafts of light streamed into the hallway. It meant only one thing. My know-it-all brother was still up—the last person I wanted to bump into on a night like this!

Tiptoeing closer, I peeked around the door. He was stuffing his face with the leftovers from supper. This could be tricky—smuggling Lissa into the house without Skip knowing.

He glanced up. "Hey, feline freak. Can't ya sleep?"

I ignored him, heading for the back door.

"Sleepwalking, Mer?" he persisted.

"What?" I muttered, pulling the curtains to one side and peering out. Skip smacked disgustingly on a meat loaf sandwich while I devised a way to distract him.

"You should be in bed," he demanded.

I whirled around. "*You're* still up!"

"Don't get smart, cat breath." Skip gulped down half a glass of milk in one swallow.

In a flash, I remembered Abednego, my wayward kitten. Genius! I turned the doorknob and stepped outside.

"Hey, close that door!" Skip yelled.

"Lost my cat," I said, pulling the door shut. Casting a fleeting glance over my shoulder, I went in search of Lissa. Around the side of the house, near a stack of firewood, I found her.

"I-I saw the l-light in the k-kitchen," she stammered. "D-Didn't want t-to—"

"C'mon, it's awful cold." I led her around to the long front porch. "Wait here—I'll go through the house and open the door."

Meow! I leaned over and spotted two shining eyes under the porch.

Then I heard Skip calling. "Merry, get your cat tail in here!"

My heart pounded as I scooped Abednego into my arms. Lifting his black, furry body to my face, I darted around the house and into the kitchen.

"That's one fat cat," Skip said, casting a scornful look my way. "Too bad you found him."

I shot him a fake smile. No time to argue; Lissa was waiting, half frozen to death on the front porch.

Cuddling Abednego, I spoke in my best baby talk.

"Hello, my pwecious little boy."

Skip groaned. "Are there any strays that *don't* live here?"

"Good-night," I snapped, turning to go. When I was safely out of Skip's sight, I dashed for the front door with Abednego still in my arms.

Lissa moaned softly as I let her in.

"Follow me," I whispered.

We sneaked up the stairs to my room. This wasn't going to be a typical sleep-over. Lissa's eyes were swollen from crying, her bottom lip cracked and bleeding. And she was limping!

TWO

Back inside my bedroom, I put Abednego down and locked the door. Lissa sat on my bed while I turned on the lamp. "I'll get something for your lip," I said, hurrying to the bathroom adjoining my room.

Lissa was pulling off her jacket and scarf when I returned with damp tissues. Her tennies were stiff from the cold.

"Here, this'll help." I gave her the wet tissues. "Careful. Don't press too hard."

She nodded as if to thank me, holding the crumpled wad on her bottom lip. Tentatively, she glanced around the room, taking note of the wall nearest her. It was covered with framed photography—some of my very best. Lissa was shaking, so I turned up the controls on the electric blanket.

"You'll warm up fast in here," I said, pulling back the blue hand-quilted comforter, a gift from my Amish neighbors down the lane.

Lissa crawled into bed, jeans and all.

I searched in the closet for my sleeping bag and rolled

it out on the floor next to the bed. "If we're quiet, Skip'll never know you're here."

Lissa looked at me sadly through the slits in her puffy eyelids. She dabbed her lip gently.

I sat on top of my sleeping bag, worried for my friend. "You're really hurt, aren't you?"

She squeaked, "Uh-huh," in an uncontrollable voice. Tears filled her eyes.

"What happened tonight?"

Her shoulders heaved under the blankets as she buried her head in my pillow. The wad of wet tissues rolled out of her hand and onto the floor.

"Talk to me, Liss," I said, kneeling up, stroking her back. I hoped her answer wasn't something truly horrible.

Minutes passed. Except for an occasional sob, the room was silent. At last, she looked at me with tearful blue eyes. "My dad got mad."

A lump clutched my throat just as Abednego jumped onto the bed. I moved the cat trio one by one on top of the little lumps made by Lissa's feet.

She eased back against the pillow. "I freak out, Merry. I freak when my dad's drunk." She wiped the tears. "I can't go home anymore."

Pulling the covers up around her chin, I tucked her in like she was a helpless little child. "Don't worry, Lissa, I'll think of something. Maybe we can talk to the school counselor tomorrow."

"I can't go to school," she blurted. "People will be looking for me."

"What people?" I sat on the edge of the bed.

"Maybe the cops," she whispered. "I'm a runaway,

aren't I?" She watched the kittens congregate at her feet.

"What about your mom? She'll be worried."

"I told her I'd leave someday." Lissa stopped momentarily.

"What about the history test? You can't skip out on *that*. Mr. Wilson's make-up tests are hideous." I was groping at thin air. Anything to talk sense into her.

She sighed. "I need your help, Merry."

"What can I do?" I whispered.

"Keep me safe." She touched me. "Please?"

I looked down at her hand on my arm. "Don't you have any relatives in Lancaster?" It was a long shot.

She shook her head.

I pulled my left earring out, glanced at it, and put it right back in. "What about your grandma?" I asked.

"She lives in Philadelphia now," Lissa said.

I pushed my hair back, taking a deep breath. Lissa was asking a lot. Especially with my parents gone. I started to speak, to set her straight about what I should and shouldn't do, but tears began to flow unchecked down her gaunt cheeks.

"Okay, Liss," I said, "but only for tonight." I clicked off the blue-and-white striped lamp on the table beside the bed, hoping I was doing the right thing.

In the darkness, my friend pleaded, "Promise to keep my secret?"

I shuddered at what it meant. If Mom and Dad were back from their mission trip, they'd know exactly what to do. I pushed my fingers through the length of my hair and crawled into my sleeping bag. A moonbeam played hide-and-seek as a cloud drifted by.

Lissa reached her hand out to me. "Merry . . . please?"

A feeling of determination flooded me as I took her cold hand in both of mine. "Don't worry. You can count on me."

I stared at a small photo on the far wall. Small, but distinct, the picture was a close-up of a gravestone covered with yellow daisies. The gravestone reminded me of another place—another time. A time when I could've helped, but didn't.

I hardly slept the rest of the night. I'd given my word to hide Lissa and keep her secret. A secret bigger than us both.

THREE

I awakened the next morning to pounding. "Get up, Merry! You're late!" Skip hollered through the door. "Don't you know people die in bed?"

I groaned, then bolted upright, glancing up from my sleeping bag. Lissa was still asleep. Thank goodness for locked bedroom doors!

"Last call, cat breath," big brother called. "Or you're history!"

History—Mr. Wilson's test! I dragged my limp legs from the sleeping bag as the events of last night came rushing back. I hurried into the bathroom adjoining my room and turned on the shower. Reaching for a clean washcloth and a bar of soap, I lathered up, remembering the first day I'd met Lissa Vyner.

It was seventh grade. Last year. I'd taken first place in the photography contest at Mifflin Middle School. Felt pretty smug about it, too. It was a high that set me sailing into second semester. That's when the new girl showed up in my class—a pretty girl—with hair the color of wheat at harvest. As for her broken arm, she'd blamed it on being accident prone.

Lissa was also quite forgetful when it came to necessary things, which I discovered after our first P.E. class together. The teacher had insisted on everyone hitting the showers, sweaty or not. But Lissa had forgotten her soap. And a hairbrush!

The next day, I came to her rescue again. This time it was a matter of life and death. She'd misplaced her red pen, and red pens were essential equipment in Miss Cassavant's math class. *"If you aren't prepared to grade your classmate's homework, you aren't prepared for life,"* the flamboyant Miss Cassavant would say.

Soon Lissa and I became good friends. Occasionally, she confided in me about her family. She felt lonely at home; hated being the only child. Lissa hated something else, too. The way her dad drank. The way it changed him. Now all of it made sense: her frequent black eyes, her broken arm . . .

A knock on the bathroom door startled me. "Thought you'd left," Lissa whispered as she crept in.

I peeked around the steamed-up shower door. "Sleep okay?"

"I think so," she said. "Mind if I use your brush?" She leaned close to the mirror, untying her yellow hair ribbon before brushing her wavy, shoulder-length hair. "It feels good being here, Mer. It's as if I have a real sister."

Grabbing my towel, I sighed, and wrapped it around me. I didn't want to think about sisters. Real or not. "I've come up with a solution," I said, changing the subject.

Lissa kept brushing her hair.

"First of all, help yourself to anything you'd like to wear in my closet while I get something for us to eat. And

. . . could you just hang out in my room today?"

Lissa nodded, holding my brush in midair.

"Now, be sure to keep the bedroom door locked just in case," I continued, reaching for my bathrobe. "We'll talk more after school, okay?" It was the best I could do on such short notice—a rather boring scheme, not the creative kind I was known for—but at least she'd be well hidden.

"What about your brother?" she asked.

I wrapped my hair in a towel. "Don't worry. Skip has intramurals on Tuesdays, so we're set."

Lissa wandered out of the bathroom over to my white corner bookcase and reached for a poetry book.

"Help yourself," I said, spying the book she held. "That one's pure genius."

"I thought only bleeding hearts read poetry."

"*I* read it," I said. "And I'm far less anguished than you think." A few strands of hair escaped, tickling my shoulders with water drops. I pushed them into the towel and investigated my wardrobe.

"Remember, don't tell anyone at school where I am, or I'm doomed!" There was desperation in Lissa's voice.

"Count on it," I said, choosing my favorite sweater, a delicious coral color. It made my chestnut brown hair and eyes look even darker. Aunt Teri had knit it for my thirteenth birthday—September 22nd—almost two months ago. Confidence exuded from the sweater. Some clothes were like that. Maybe it was because Aunt Teri, creative and lovely, was completely deaf. Anyway, I needed this sweater today, for more than one reason.

Lissa sat on my bed, paging through the poetry book.

Just then Abednego raised his sleepy head and made a beeline for my friend. "Hey," she said, giggling, "look at you, big guy." She patted his head.

"He's super picky about his friends." I watched in amazement as Abednego let her hold him.

"I know just what you need," she said carrying him into the bathroom. When they came out, Abednego was wearing Lissa's yellow hair ribbon around his chubby neck.

"You look very handsome," Lissa cooed into his ear. Then she put him down, headed back into the bathroom, and closed the door.

"Boy cats don't wear hair ribbons," I muttered, quite puzzled at Abednego's obvious interest in Lissa.

The phone rang and I hurried down the hallway to Skip's room.

"How's every little thing today?" came the scratchy voice as I answered the phone.

The voice belonged to Miss Spindler, our neighbor around the corner. Mom had asked her to check on us while they were gone. And check up, she did. In fact, the last few days she'd been calling nonstop, showing up nearly every evening with some rich, exotic dessert.

"We're fine, thanks," I reassured her.

"Anything you need?" came the next question.

I thought of Lissa. I'd be crazy to let Miss Spindler in on our little secret. "I think we're set here, but thanks," I said, discouraging her from coming over today.

"Well, just give a holler if you think of anything you need."

"Okay, I will . . . if we need anything." I hung up the

phone, heading back to the bedroom. "I need my hair dryer, Lissa," I called through a crack in the bathroom door.

No answer. I paused, waiting for her reply.

"Lissa, you okay?" I knocked and waited a moment, then lightly touched the door. Slowly, it opened to reveal ugly welts and bruises on Lissa's right thigh. I cringed in horror.

Startled, she tried to cover up her leg.

"I-I'm sorry," I said. Silence hung between us, then she started to cry. Deep, heart-wrenching sobs.

I ached for Lissa. "How did this happen?" I asked, squelching my shock.

"You'll never believe it." She kept her head down.

"Try me, Liss."

"I fell down the steps."

Anger swelled inside me. Not toward her, but toward whoever had done this. "Now, how about the truth," I whispered.

Wincing, she stood up. "It's a long, long story."

"I should call our family doctor." I leaned on the doorknob, hurting for my friend.

"Right, and I'll end up in some lousy foster home. No thanks, I've already been *that* route."

The impact of her words sent my mind reeling. "A foster home?"

"Two years ago." She said it through clenched teeth.

"What happened?"

"What do you think?" She sighed. "Now things are even worse with my dad at the police department. He's got every one of those cops fooled."

I didn't know what to say. Lissa's father was a cop, and cops were supposed to be the *good* guys.

Lissa's words interrupted my thoughts. "If caseworkers get involved," she added, "they'll eventually send me back home, and he'll beat me up again."

My throat turned to cotton.

"I hate my dad." Tears spilled down her cheek. "And Mom, too, for not making it stop."

I wanted to wave a wand and make things better for my friend. "I'm so sorry," I said, determined more than ever to take care of her.

Abruptly, she stood up, reaching for the shower door. "He'll never hit me again." By the cold stiffness in her voice, I knew the conversation was over.

FOUR

Frustrated and terribly worried, I mentioned breakfast. Lissa needed something nourishing, but I only had enough time to grab some juice and sticky buns.

While in the kitchen, I filled the cats' dishes with their favorite tuna food. They crowded around, nosing their way into the breakfast delight.

I washed my hands before putting three sticky buns—two for Lissa, one for me—and two glasses of orange juice on a tray. Then I headed up the back stairs.

Lissa was sitting on the bed admiring my wall gallery when I came in the room. "When did you start taking pictures?" She studied a tall picture of a willow tree in the springtime.

I set the tray down on the bed. "I won a cheap camera for selling the most Girl Scout cookies in first grade," I explained. "Taking pictures started out as a hobby, but somehow it's become an obsession."

"Your shots are great," she said, reaching for a glass of juice.

I gathered up my books and found my camera lying on the desk near the window.

"Taking more pictures today?" she asked.

"I like to have my camera handy at all times. You never know when a picture might present itself."

A pensive smile crossed Lissa's face.

"Let's pray before I catch the bus," I suggested.

Lissa seemed surprised. "Why?"

"Because I care about you. And God does, too."

She smiled weakly, then nodded her consent.

After the prayer, Lissa wiped her eyes. "That was sweet, Merry. My grandmother talks to God, too. I wish I could be more like her . . . and you."

"I don't always do the right thing." *After all, how smart is harboring a runaway?* "Don't forget to lock this door when I leave." I grabbed the sticky bun and bit into the sugary dough. Then I washed it down with a long drink of orange juice. My mother would worry if she knew I hadn't had a full breakfast today. Oh well, what was one day?

I glanced in the mirror again. "Maybe we should call your grandmother after school. Someone in your family ought to know you're safe."

"I guess I should call," Lissa agreed. "But I don't want Grandma to know where I am."

I thought of the years of abuse Lissa must have endured and nodded my consent.

"You're a true friend, Merry." She sat on my bed like a wistful statue as I turned to go.

❧ ❧

The school bus was crowded and noisy as usual. I slid in beside Chelsea Davis, another friend from school. She glanced up momentarily, said, "Hey, Mer," then resumed her frantic cramming.

Her thick auburn hair hung halfway down her back on one side. It nearly covered her face on the side facing me. I pulled back the curtain of her shining tresses. "Wilson's test?" I asked, smiling.

"You got it." She didn't look up.

Kids jostled against the seats and the doors swooshed shut. Ignoring the clamor, I centered my thoughts on Lissa's hideous bruises. Why hadn't she told me before about her abusive father? I shivered, thinking about the horrible scenes at Lissa's house, surely multiplied many times over. Outraged, I was determined to protect Lissa. Or to somehow get her linked up with her Philadelphia grandmother, the one who talked to God.

Staring out the window, I watched the familiar landmarks on SummerHill Lane. Thick rows of graceful willows separated our property from the Zooks, our Amish neighbors. Acres of rich farmland stretched away from the dirt road. A white fence surrounded their pasture. Near Abe Zooks' brick farmhouse, one of his horses, Apple, was being hitched up to a gray buggy.

We zipped past a field of drying brown cornstalks. The oldest Zook boys, Curly John and Levi, were working the field, harvesting the remaining stalks with a mule-drawn corn picker.

I snapped out of my daze when I saw Levi. Tall and just sixteen, Levi was the cutest Amish boy around. I'd saved his life once. He nearly drowned in the pond out behind our houses when his foot got caught on some willow roots. It happened the year after my own personal tragedy, when I was eight and Levi was eleven. But in my mind, it was as clear as yesterday.

"I'll get myself hitched up with you some day, Merry Hanson," Levi Zook had said. I figured he had beans for brains, since the Amish church forbids baptized Amish from marrying "English," as they called us non-Amish folk.

I leaned toward the window, accidentally bumping Chelsea. She glanced up, half-snorting when she spied Levi. "I guess you wanna hand sew all your clothes and survive without electricity for the rest of your life."

"Not me," I said, backing away from the window.

Farther down the lane, we passed the old cemetery where gravestones lay scattered across a tree-lined meadow. *Stark and lonely.* A lump sprang up in my throat, but I forced it down, purposely looking away.

As we neared the end of the lane, a group of Amish kids, two on scooters, all carrying lunch boxes, waited at the intersection. One boy caught my eye and smiled a toothless grin under the shadow of his black felt hat. It was Aaron Zook, Levi's little brother. I waved.

The bus came to a grinding stop, and the Amish kids crossed, heading for the one-room schoolhouse a half mile away. The older girls held hands with little brothers and sisters as our school bus waited. It set my thoughts spinning back to Lissa. She had no big sister or brother to look after her. Being an only child had to be tough, especially in an abusive family. Waves of worry rushed over me.

At school, I scurried to my locker, wondering how I

could concentrate on Mr. Wilson's test with Lissa in such a mess.

Unloading my things, I spied Jonathan Klein coming toward me, wearing a heart-stopping grin. A perpetual honor student, Jonathan always snagged top grades in Mr. Wilson's class. *He* looked confident enough.

"Merry, mistress of mirth. Ready for Mr. Wilson's wonderful world of terrible, tough, terminal tests?"

I scanned the history outline one last time. "Tearfully trying," I replied, playing our little game.

"Good going." He laughed. "Can you beat this one? Every eventful historical example ends up on Mr. Wilson's engaging exams." The Alliteration Wizard was two jumps ahead of me. His brown eyes sparkled. Looked like he'd had a full night's sleep. No runaways in *his* closet.

I accompanied him to his locker and tried to conjure up a clever response. Then it spilled out, "Each enormous expanse of energy excites brain cells—" I caught my breath.

Way at the end of the hallway, a police officer—Lissa's father—was marching through the crowd of students. Heading straight for me!

"Jon, quick! Stand in front of me," I said, squeezing into his open locker.

"What're you doing?" His eyes filled with questions.

"Fake it!" I whispered through clenched teeth. "Pretend you're hanging up your jacket." My heart thumped so loud I just knew the noise would lead Mr. Vyner straight to his target. Me!

FIVE

I held my breath as seconds sauntered by. At last, I peered through Jonathan's jacket. "The coast is clear."

He looked puzzled. "What was that all about?"

"Say it with all *p*'s," I said, hurrying to first period history class.

He slammed his locker door. "Hey, not so fast!"

I brushed my hair back and rushed through the hall, cautiously looking in all directions.

Is Mr. Vyner gone? I wondered.

Sneaking around the corner, I made a detour to survey the school office. Yee-ikes! There sat Lissa's father, waiting for the principal.

I could see it now. Mr. Vyner would ask the principal for the names of her best friends. Maybe even call them out of class. *"Merry Hanson, please come to the school office. . . ."*

Pins and needles pricked my conscience, and I spent the rest of the day on the verge of hysteria waiting to hear my name over the intercom.

After school, I scrambled onto the school bus. Sliding in beside Chelsea, I tried to avoid Jonathan by scooting down in my seat. When he boarded the bus, I lowered my head.

"Hiding from someone?" Chelsea whispered, giggling.

"Sh-h!"

"He's coming," she teased.

Jon planted himself in front of us, leaning his arm on the back of the seat. His light brown hair was brushed back on the sides and a cream-colored shirt peeked out of his open jacket. "You can't ignore me all day," he said.

I sat up and pulled a snack-size bag of chips out of my schoolbag. I shot glances at Jon while Chelsea smirked knowingly.

Persistence, a fine trait for a fine guy. And fine was putting it mildly. "That was some history test," I said.

"You're changing the subject," Jon replied.

"What?"

Chelsea pretended to choke. I poked her in the ribs as my handsome interrogator grinned, waiting for an answer.

I sighed. "Things are blurry, bleary, blue. Sorry, I can't share 'em with you."

Jonathan's brown eyes grew serious. "Coming to the church hayride tonight? Everyone will be there."

Our eyes locked. "I can't." It was a hayride not to be missed. Full moon; good times. Too bad Jonathan only thought of me as a friend.

His smile warmed my heart. "The hay wagon's coming right down SummerHill Lane, past your house," he persisted. "We could stop and pick you up."

"I'm sorry, really." I hoped he'd let it drop.

The bus slowed to a crawl as we came up on a horse and buggy. The Amish man sat in the front seat on the right, holding the reins. His wife sat on the left. Two cherub-faced girls stared over the backseat from beneath black bonnets.

"It's the Yoders," Chelsea said, shoving her knees up against the back of the seat. "My mom drives Mr. Yoder and his business partner to town every day."

The kids behind us jumped up for a better look. "Why don't they just buy a car?" one boy taunted. "Those old buggies are tearing up the roads."

"Relax," Jon told the boy, who was new to the Lancaster area. "They'll be turning off soon." And in a few minutes they did.

The bus sped down the lane past the Amish farms, to my house, one of the few non-Amish residences on the three-mile stretch. The bus groaned to a halt, sending a cloud of dust swirling as I hopped out.

Eager to get back to Lissa, I made a quick stop at the mailbox. Its contents almost spilled out with tons of important-looking mail. A letter from Aunt Teri and Uncle Pete caught my eye.

Dashing into the house, I dumped Dad's mail on the hall table. Then checking for any early signs of Skip, I raced upstairs.

"Lissa, I'm home," I called, digging into my jeans pocket for the key to my bedroom.

Inside, I discovered Lissa asleep on my unmade bed, the book of poems open on the floor. The cat trio bounded into the bedroom, nosing their way into my hands as I sat on the floor watching my sleeping friend. I rubbed Abednego's black neck. His gentle purring rose to a rumble. I smiled at the yellow ribbon on his neck, the one Lissa had tied there this morning.

"You look beautiful, little boy," I whispered, hugging him. As usual, Shadrach and Meshach fought for equal time. Once they were settled, I leaned back and pulled my baby album out of the rack on my desk. Opening to the beginning, I found the pages I loved most—the first seven birthdays of my life. I smiled at the photos, fingering the shoulder strap on my camera still in the schoolbag beside me.

The phone's jangling made me jump. I closed the album and pushed the cats out of my lap. Running down the hall to Skip's room, I hoped the phone wouldn't awaken Lissa. It was probably Miss Spindler calling to check on "every little thing."

I picked up the phone. "Hanson residence."

"Is this Merry Hanson . . . on SummerHill Lane?"

My hands perspired. The man's voice sounded familiar. "Who's calling please?" I asked without revealing my identity, the way my parents had instructed.

"This is Lissa Vyner's father. I wonder if you might be able to help me?"

My fingers squeezed the receiver. My lips and throat turned to cotton. Swallowing, I prayed silently, *Lord, help me!* Then I took a deep breath. "How can I help you?" I said, scared he'd hear the quiver in my voice.

He continued, "Lissa is missing and her mother and

I are gathering information from her friends. Have you seen her by any chance?"

I hesitated. What would happen if I said the wrong thing and gave away Lissa's secret?

Fierce pounding came to my heart, but I spoke slowly. "Yes, I've seen Lissa."

"Where? When?" the frantic questions came.

"Yesterday at school," I replied. It was the truth, at least part of it. Still, I felt guilty.

"Did she say anything to you about running away?"

"No, sir." Again, the truth. But my deceitful words haunted me.

"Well, if you happen to see or hear from her again, I'd appreciate it very much if you'd give me a call. Thank you, Merry. Goodbye."

Confused, I hung up the phone. Lissa's father had always treated me cordially the few times I'd visited there. Now he sounded concerned, almost panic-stricken. Not like a child-beater.

I hurried down the hall to my bedroom. Lissa was stretching her arms and yawning as I came in. She sat up, her eyes still puffy and her bottom lip slightly swollen.

"How'd you sleep?" I plopped down on a shaggy rug near the bed.

"I dreamed my dad was out looking for me."

"He *is* looking for you."

She gasped. "At school?"

I nodded.

"Merry, you didn't talk to him, you didn't—"

"I promised, remember? But . . ."

"But what? Tell me!" Her cheeks were flushed and she

leaned forward as if her whole world dangled on a thread.

"Everything's fine, trust me," I began. "But your father just called here a few minutes ago. He sounds very worried."

Lissa pounded her fist into my comforter. "He knows how to do that. Don't you see, Merry? He changes. He fools people!"

The desperate feeling returned. This time it was a jerking, twisting knot deep in the pit of my stomach.

SIX

I studied my friend. "Please, Lissa, let's talk to a professional—"

"You don't know what you're saying," she interrupted. "The school counselor can't help my dad. No one can!" Her eyes glistened. "We've been through all this before."

"Why didn't you tell me?"

Lissa's lips were set. "It's not that easy to talk about."

"And it's hard for me to relate," I whispered. "I'm sorry." Glancing at my blue-striped wall clock, I thought of the long-distance call she needed to make. "It's almost four. We've got about an hour before Skip shows up. Why don't you call your grandmother now?"

Lissa looked at me, tears coming fast.

"Stay here. I'll get the portable phone." I ran downstairs to my dad's study. Poor Lissa. Things just had to work out for her.

Back upstairs, I offered to leave while she made her call. "You could use some privacy," I said.

"No, I can be alone any old time," she replied, punching the numbers on the receiver. "It feels good having you here."

Seconds passed. Then she spoke, "Hi, Grandma, it's Lissa. I miss you like crazy." She sounded sugary sweet. I couldn't help noticing the change in her countenance. It was obvious Lissa loved her grandmother. Trusted her, too.

I sat at my desk, studying Aunt Teri's unopened letter. The words *The Hanson Family* jumped out at me, so I tore the envelope open.

Then without warning, Lissa was sobbing. "I want you to come get me, Grandma," she pleaded. "I can't go back home."

There was a long pause. Her grandmother was probably trying to comfort her. Maybe arranging transportation.

Then I heard, "No, they don't know where I am. Can't you please come?"

I held the letter in my hand, waiting breathlessly for the response. But there was only more pleading from Lissa. My heart throbbed with worry. What if Lissa's grandmother couldn't help?

"It's no use," Lissa cried into the receiver. "Dad's a cop; the police department only sees his *good* side. They'll never believe me, Grandma. You've got to help me!"

It didn't sound like Lissa's grandmother was going to budge. Now I knew for sure I was in over my head.

Silently, I prayed, *Dear Lord, please help Lissa out of this mess. And help me, too. I want to do the right thing.*

While Lissa continued to talk through her tears, I began to read Aunt Teri's letter. My eyes stopped on the second sentence. I shook my head. "Just what we don't need," I muttered.

Aunt Teri and Uncle Pete were coming to Lancaster on Wednesday night—tomorrow!

I looked up to see Lissa pushing the antenna into the phone as she scooted off the bed. "Grandma's got her own ideas," she complained. "I guess she just doesn't want to get involved this time."

Exasperated, I slipped the letter back in the envelope. "So she's helped you out before?"

"Yeah, but this time she told me to call my mom."

"Sounds like a winner," I replied.

Lissa turned to me, looking horror-stricken. "How can you say that? After everything?"

I stood up, hands on my hips. "I want you to tell me everything, Lissa, starting with last night. Tell me exactly what happened."

She glared at me. "So now you think it's *my* fault." Two giant tears spilled down her cheeks.

"I never said it was your fault, Lissa. I just want you to level with me."

"You won't believe me anyway," she scoffed.

"Whoa, wait a minute. I don't deserve that and you know it," I shot back. "Your grandmother believes you, and she thinks you should call your mother. I happen to agree with her. Rethink what your grandmother just said."

"Oh, no you don't. I'm not calling my mom and that's final." Defiance laced her words.

"Your mom deserves to know you're safe, Liss. *I'll* call her."

Lissa shook her head. "You can't do that. We have one of those machines that tells the phone number and the name of the person calling."

I groaned. "What about the abuse hotline on TV? You can call them without giving your name."

"They can trace calls from the hotline," she said. "Besides, my dad goes on duty pretty soon. I can't take any chances."

I wished my parents were here. "So much for that idea," I mumbled, thinking about my mother. *What would she do if she were me?*

To begin with, Mom wouldn't have promised Lissa she'd keep her secret. She was smart that way—didn't let people push her into a corner. I missed her now more than ever.

Lissa leaned back against the pillows on my bed, looking thin and frail. She scarcely filled out my clothes, even though we were the same height. "There's something you don't know," she began. The tone of her voice had changed. Deep and sad. "It's about my mother."

I shivered, not sure I wanted to know more.

"My dad hits her, too," she said softly. The truth hung heavily between us. "Mom knows all about abuse. But if she can't help herself, how can she help me?"

Her words cut through me. I sighed. "I know someone who can help."

Lissa leaned up on her elbow, an eager look in her eyes.

"My dad's a doctor." I sat on the bed. "He's good friends with this lawyer who goes to our church. My parents'll be home on Thursday—if I can hide you out till then, I guarantee they'll help us."

"That's only two days away," she said, looking more hopeful.

"But there's a problem. My aunt and uncle are coming tomorrow, on their way to Pittsburgh."

Lissa looked as frantic as her father sounded on the phone. "What'll we do?"

"Don't worry, I have an idea." I slipped my hair behind my ear, thinking about a plan to hide her. "But there's something we should talk about first."

"What?"

I pulled my camera out of my schoolbag. "This."

"I don't get it." She looked totally confused. "What's the camera for?"

"Your bruises might start fading before my dad gets back," I said. "He'll need documented proof."

Lissa groaned.

"It won't be so bad," I assured her as she exposed the bruise on her thigh. "Now hold still." I took several good close-up shots of her leg, then her swollen lip.

When the cap on the lens was secure, Lissa limped over to my walk-in closet. She opened the door and hobbled inside. "I could hide in here, easy," she announced with a face full of sunshine.

She's desperate, I decided. The closet was spacious, but hardly big enough to set up housekeeping. "It won't work. My aunt and uncle always stay in this room when they come."

A disappointed look replaced her sunny countenance. "What about your parents' room?"

Out of the question. "It's just too risky, but don't

worry. I think I know what we can do. C'mon, let's grab a snack. You're hungry, right?"

I helped Lissa down the stairs. She moved slowly, one step at a time. "What's your plan?" she asked.

"I have to work some things out first," I said, holding out my hand to her at the bottom of the staircase.

When we arrived in the kitchen, she stared at the wallpaper. "Your mom must like strawberries." She traced the outline of leaves on the wall.

I laughed, glancing at the strawberry clock and cookie jar to match. "We don't live on the corner of Strawberry Lane and SummerHill for nothing!"

She looked at me. "Merry, merry strawberry," Lissa rhymed.

"Hey, I like that." I got sandwich fixings out of the fridge. "Did I ever tell you how I got my name?"

Lissa shook her head, leaning her elbows on the oval table.

"My parents said I didn't cry when I was born. I laughed!" I spread mayonnaise over two pieces of bread.

She chuckled. "Brain damage?"

"Probably. Mom says they named me just right because I'm a happy person."

Lissa's face turned solemn. "Then I must've bawled my eyes out when I was born, because I've been crying ever since."

"Ham and cheese sandwich comin' up," I announced, ignoring her morbid comment.

She pulled the bread apart and peered inside. "Where're the pickles?"

"Who's boss around here anyway?"

Her face lit up. "You're wonderful, Merry," she said. "Wouldn't it be fun if we could be sisters somehow?" She bit into her sandwich while I poured a glass of milk for each of us.

So *that's* what Lissa wanted. Not to run away from a family, but to belong to one. Really and truly belong.

I slid the pickle jar out of the fridge. "I had a sister once. A twin sister."

A frown appeared on Lissa's face.

"Faithie died of leukemia when we were seven. It seems so long ago, it's hard to know if my memories of her come from pictures and what my parents say, or if they're my own." I cut a pickle lengthwise.

"Did she look like you?" Lissa asked.

"We weren't identical twins, if that's what you mean, but everyone said we had the same eyes." I paused, handing her the pickle slices. "I miss her. Every day of my life."

Suddenly, a knock came at the back door. Lissa leaped off her chair, almost falling. Panic shot out of her eyes like an animal caught in a deadly trap. "Remember— you haven't seen me!" And she limped off toward the hall closet.

SEVEN

When Lissa was safely out of sight, I went to the back door and pushed the curtain back. Outside, a friendly face smiled at me. It was Rachel Zook. She held a basket of fresh eggs in her gloved hands.

I opened the door. "Hi, Rachel."

She smiled. "Hello, Merry. Fresh eggs for my English cousin."

I brightened at her warm greeting. Rachel thought of me as a close friend because our family trees branched back to the same ancestors. She called me "English" because I wasn't Amish.

"Thanks to Skip's giant omelets, we're all out of eggs." I took the basket from her. "He uses up twice the eggs Mom does." And with that, I went to find the egg money in the utensil drawer.

Rachel twinkled a smile. "Come on over for Curly John's wedding on Thursday, *jah?*"

"Wouldn't miss it," I said, feeling rude about not inviting her inside.

"Curly John wants all of you to come," Rachel said. She adjusted the black woolen shawl draped over her shoulders. It was fastened in front with a safety pin.

Curly John was Rachel's nineteen-year-old brother. Two years older than Skip. I couldn't imagine *my* brother getting married, tending a farm, and raising a family at that age.

"Mother and Daddy won't be home till Thursday night, but Skip and I can come for sure."

Rachel pushed a strand of light brown hair back under her black winter bonnet. "Such good fun, weddings." She turned to go.

"Thanks for the invitation," I called after her.

She waved. "*Wilkom*, Merry."

I watched as Rachel hurried past the white gazebo in our backyard. The deep purple skirt whipped against her ankles, covered with black cotton stockings. "Please don't misunderstand, dear friend," I whispered, leaning against the door, wishing I'd taken a chance and invited her in.

Remembering Lissa, I dashed to the hall closet and opened the door. "Come finish your sandwich."

"Who was that?" Lissa asked, moving out from behind the vacuum cleaner.

"Rachel Zook, my Amish friend."

Lissa eased herself into a kitchen chair. "Do I know her?"

"She lives down the lane." I pointed in the direction, still hoping I hadn't offended Rachel. "She goes to a one-room Amish school."

Lissa drank some milk. "What grade?"

"She's in eighth, but this is her last year."

Lissa's eyebrows shot up. "She's dropping out?"

"Amish only go eight grades. After that, they get ready to settle down and marry."

"At fourteen?"

"That's when some of them start running around, hanging out with friends like we do. Except they get together on Sunday nights, at singings. It's where guys meet girls."

"While they're singing?" Lissa's eyes were as big as windows.

"They sit around a long table with boys on one side and girls on the other. And . . . guess what else?"

Lissa snickered. "Can't wait to hear this."

"Adults aren't allowed."

"So what?" Lissa stared at me. "Doesn't sound like much fun anyway."

I got up and looked out the window. "The Amish teens pick out fast hymns and sing for a couple hours. Sometimes it turns into a square dance, but it's not supposed to."

"How come?"

"The older Amish don't want their teens dancing." I peeked out the back window again, watching for Skip's return. "Sometimes they have secret dances and disobey *Gelassenheit* anyhow."

Lissa frowned hard. "Gelassen-what?"

"It means submission, obedience to the Amish community."

"How do you know all this Amish stuff?"

"You won't believe it," I said. "Rachel and I traced our ancestors back to Switzerland to the original Amish immigrants. They sailed together on *The Charming Nancy* in 1737."

"What a cool name for a ship."

"Cool, but slow," I told her. "It took eighty-three days to finally dock in Philadelphia."

"So why aren't you Amish?" Lissa asked before taking the last bite of sandwich.

"One of my great-grandfathers pulled away from the Amish faith." I glanced at the strawberry clock on the wall, keeping track of time before Skip's arrival. I went to the sink, which was still piled with dishes from his marathon midnight snack. Slowly, I opened the dishwasher.

Lissa took another sip of milk, then set the glass down firmly. "Somehow I can't picture you being friends with a girl like Rachel Zook."

She sounded jealous, but I let it go. I'd heard that sometimes abused kids are insecure. Lissa was probably suffering from a lot of things like that. As her friend, it was my job to protect her, not judge her.

After scraping the dishes, I loaded the dishwasher. "I really think you'd like Rachel, if you got to know her."

"You see beauty in everything, Merry. Maybe it's the photographer in you." She looked depressed again. "What's wrong with *me*?"

I turned the dial on the dishwasher. "Nothing's wrong, Lissa."

She sat up. "I love the guitar. I had one before we moved here, but my dad sold it out from under my nose." She paused for a moment, as though reliving a sad moment. Then she asked, "Ever make up a melody?"

I breathed deeply. "No, but Jonathan Klein has."

"Your boyfriend, right?"

I wiped the crumbs off the counter. "Oh, he's nice enough."

"C'mon, Merry, I know you like him!" She leaned back in her chair and squinted at me. "But I still can't believe a guy would propose to a girl based on her singing."

"Let's face it, Liss, if you were Amish, you'd be livin' for Sunday nights."

We burst into giggles.

Just then I heard the front door open. I grabbed Lissa's arm and whispered, "Quick! Upstairs!"

It was slow going for Lissa, but we managed to get up the back steps. Like frightened mice, we scurried to my room.

EIGHT

"In there," I whispered, pointing to my walk-in closet. Lissa pulled me inside with her. "For how long?"

"What?"

"C'mon, Mer, you say 'what' when you don't know what else to say."

"Hardly ever," I huffed.

Lissa sat cross-legged in the middle of the closet floor, straightening a row of shoe boxes. "Did you know you have six of these?" It was obvious she didn't want me to leave yet.

"Take a peek." I motioned to the shoe boxes.

Hesitantly, she opened the first one and discovered a plastic bag brimful of granola. Sliding the lid off the second shoe box, Lissa stared in amazement at a variety of fruit leather.

"What's your favorite flavor?" I asked, hoping to dispel her dismal mood.

She looked puzzled. "What's fruit leather doing in a shoe box?"

"It's shoe leather replacement." I laughed. "Let me introduce you to my snack pantry." I popped the lid off the third shoe box, revealing a plastic container of powdery Kool-Aid. "Care for a lick?"

Lissa smiled. "You're crazy."

"I always get hungry when I do homework, so I stash food in my closet," I said, offering her a strip of apple fruit leather. "You can snack till I smuggle dinner up."

Her face lit up. "How can I ever thank you?" she said. And I knew it had little to do with the fruit leather.

"Hm-m, let's see," I said. "How about that new down-filled jacket of yours? Think you could loan it?"

"No problem."

I studied Lissa, helpless and forlorn, sitting there on the floor of my closet. "You'd really let me?"

She nodded. "Except it's at my house."

I pretended to be disappointed. "Oh, phooey."

Lissa brightened. "I have an idea. You could sneak into my house and get it tomorrow afternoon."

"What?"

"Mom works Wednesdays all day, and Daddy, well, he'll be asleep. Or—" She sighed.

"Or what?" I asked.

Lissa gave a piercing look. "Drunk," she said, slowly. "He'll be drunk." Tears spilled down her cheeks, and I couldn't help but put my arm around her, even though I felt sad inside, too. But I needed to be merry and strong. For Lissa.

"You okay?" I asked.

She shook her head, and I tried to picture her situation at home. Coming from a background of loving parents, it wasn't easy. I stood up. "I'll be right back, okay?"

"Promise?" She looked at me with pleading eyes.

"Count on it," I said.

❧　　❧

Downstairs, I hurried into the kitchen. Skip was moving things around in the freezer, obviously searching for just the right casserole. He must've sensed I was observing him, because he straightened up and with a grand flourish, whipped out one of the frozen casseroles Mom had prepared in advance. "Tah-dah!" he shouted.

I giggled. "What's for supper?"

"Wouldn't *you* like to know?"

"C'mon, I'm starved," I said, settling down into one of the kitchen chairs. I watched him set the oven and loosen the aluminum foil on the casserole dish.

"How was your history test?" he asked.

Mr. Wilson's terrible, terminal test, as Jonathan had described it, seemed so far away now. I took a deep breath. "It was . . . well, I guess I should've studied more," I admitted.

Skip cast a hard look at me. "It might help if you studied instead of chasing orphan cats all night."

"Don't exaggerate," I said, tossing Aunt Teri's letter on the table. "Guess who's coming to visit?"

Skip's shoulders drooped. "Don't people know Mom and Dad are overseas?" He took a quick look at the letter, then a smile spread across his face. "Hey, this could be a blessing in disguise."

A blessing for him, I thought, wondering how to make my scheme to hide Lissa work.

"Aunt Teri cooks like nobody's business," he said.

"Food—is that all you ever think about?"

He poured milk into a tall glass. "You'd better get your room ready, little girl." He lifted the glass to his lips and gulped down half the contents.

"Yeah, yeah." I reached for the tablet of instruction notes Mom had left on top of the fridge.

Playfully, Skip grabbed the notebook from me and scanned the list of events, holding it higher and higher, playing keep-away. "Hey, we're in luck," he said. "The cleaning lady comes first thing tomorrow."

I jumped up and grabbed the tablet out of his hands. "Let me see that."

Skip muttered something about little sisters with cat breath. I stared at the list, making a mental note to tell Lissa about the housekeeper.

My brother nosed around in the refrigerator. He spotted the fresh eggs from Zooks' farm. "Looks like Rachel was here."

"Which reminds me," I said. "Don't forget, we're going to Curly John's wedding on Thursday."

"An Amish wedding feast? I'll be there!" He pulled the basket of eggs out of the fridge. "Hey, Mer, how about one of my omelet specials?"

"Oh, ick. I'd eat Mom's casseroles rock hard before—"

"That does it!" Skip grabbed a tea towel and flipped it around, winding it up for a good cracking.

I dodged the flicks of his towel.

CRA-A-ACK!

"I love your omelets, Skip. Honest!"

"Say it louder," he demanded as a mischievous grin slid across his face.

I ran behind the table, away from my power-crazed brother. "I wish Mom and Dad could see you now," I shouted. "Then they'd never leave me alone with you!" He chased me around the kitchen, and when I passed the window, I noticed a police car pulling into our driveway.

"Skip, look! Cops!"

"I never fall for that trick," he said, coming after me. But when I didn't move, he stopped in front of the window and we both stared out at a white patrol car. "What's this about?" he said.

My heart pounded *Lissa, Lissa, Lissa* ninety miles an hour.

NINE

"Wow, I hope this isn't about Mom and Dad!" Skip said as the doorbell rang. He went to answer it while I dashed up the back steps, my heart in my throat.

I tore into my bedroom. "Lissa!" I opened the closet door and looked around. She was nowhere in sight. "Lissa?"

Silence.

"C'mon, Liss, where *are* you?" I turned around, closing the closet door behind me. I thought back to my last conversation with her. "What have I done?" I said out loud. *I should've known better than to leave her alone, crying.*

I scrambled to my desk, looking for a note. *Anything.* Glancing out the window, I saw another policeman. This one was standing like a guard out front.

Maybe it was a stakeout. And maybe I was a suspect. I cringed, wondering how I'd gotten myself into such a horrible mess. What if the police had a search warrant?

And what about poor Lissa? Visions of foster homes or maybe more parental abuse crisscrossed my mind. Where was she now? Had she run away—again?

"Merry!" Skip called from downstairs. "Come here a minute."

"Lord, help me," I whispered, making my way down the long staircase, holding the railing for dear life.

Skip stood in the entryway talking to a tall, heavyset policeman. They turned to face me as I reached the bottom of the steps.

"Merry, this is Officer Rhodes," Skip said. "Did you know Lissa Vyner is missing?"

I held my breath to keep from saying the wrong thing as the policeman shoved his identification under my nose. "I'd like to talk with you, Merry, if that's all right."

I nodded and Skip led the way into the living room. It bugged me how my big brother seemed so eager to accept this unwelcome guest. I took Mother's overstuffed chair across from Officer Rhodes. It was as comforting as her arms might have been, if only she were here. Abednego leaped up, searching for a comfortable spot on my lap.

"I'm sorry to bother you like this, Merry, with your parents gone and all," he said in a voice as stiff as the way he sat on the edge of our green paisley sofa. Looking puzzled, Skip perched himself on the matching ottoman.

I felt the policeman's eyes studying me, so I managed to say, "Is everything okay?" My voice seemed to spell out g-u-i-l-t-y.

"We certainly hope so," the policeman said. "But it appears that Lissa Vyner has run away and since you're one of her friends, her parents thought you might be able to help."

I looked him in the eyes, stroking my cat's neck to beat

the band, wondering what kind of man he'd be if he discovered Lissa hiding upstairs. His gray eyes looked kind enough. And his chin was firm and strong, but it was a chin that meant business, and from the way Skip leaned forward, I knew they were both waiting for an answer.

"Has Lissa called you? Have you talked to her?" Officer Rhodes asked.

I gave him the most innocent look I had and hoped it was good enough. Steady, non-blinking eyes are supposed to make a person look trustworthy. I'd read that somewhere.

I was determined not to lie, unless . . .

"Merry!" Skip urged. "Tell him if you know something."

"Well, yes, sir," I admitted.

"Has Lissa called here?" the officer asked.

"Well, no, not called, really . . ."

Skip was beside himself. "Out with it, Mer. Did she call or didn't she?"

I wanted to hide from Skip's accusing eyes. It was one thing to see questions in the policeman's eyes, but quite another to see them in my brother's.

I thought of Lissa. She certainly wasn't anywhere to be seen last time I looked upstairs. It wouldn't be a lie to say I didn't know where she was—at least not at the moment.

"Lissa's dad beat her up," I said glumly.

"So you *have* heard from her?" Officer Rhodes asked. His eagerness irritated me. I nodded.

"Do you know where she is?"

"No." I shook my head. *Not anymore,* I thought. And that was the truth!

The sound of static, followed by a muffled voice, came over Officer Rhodes' pager. Abruptly, he stood to his feet, answering it as he did. He seemed taller than before, and I kept shooting my most innocent look up at him, while I wore out Abednego's neck rubbing it.

Seconds passed, uncomfortable seconds. How much longer?

Finally, he hooked the pager back onto his belt. "Thanks for your time, young lady." His gaze dropped to my cat.

"You're welcome, sir." I watched his face as he stared at Abednego. Gently, I lifted my black cat down. That's when I put two and two together. I swallowed hard as Officer Rhodes studied the yellow hair ribbon tied around Abednego's neck. It was Lissa's!

Without another word, the policeman headed for the front door with Skip on his heels. I stayed frozen to my mother's chair while Skip showed the nosy cop out. I didn't care to hear what else he said to my brother, but after he left, Skip marched back in.

"I don't figure you, Mer." He sat down. For the first time in ages, his face had a stern coolness to it, not like the half-mischievous, half-stern looks I usually got. The ones he could turn on and off whenever he pleased.

I was silent.

Skip stood up. "Well, if you happen to see Lissa or hear from her again, be sure to call this number." He flicked the officer's card at me. "If her dad did beat her, she needs help."

I picked it up, feeling horribly guilty about my deceit. It was time for the truth. Whether Lissa liked it or not. But first, I had to find her.

Upstairs, I locked my bedroom door and sat down, wondering how Lissa could've made the slip. She was nowhere in this room. Or the closet.

Then, out of the stillness, I heard a soft giggle. I flung the closet door wide and listened. "Lissa?"

Another giggle drifted out from the hanging clothes on the left side of my closet. Whirling around, I stared. "Lissa, you in here?"

"Inside your winter coat."

I stared in disbelief. A pair of fashion boots were sticking out of my long red coat. "What are you doing? Didn't you hear me calling you?"

Her face stuck out, flushed from the warmth of my coat. "I heard the doorbell. What's going on downstairs?"

"I think your dad's on to us."

Lissa gasped. "Help me out of here."

"The police are looking for you," I said. "They were just here."

Wide-eyed and breathing fast, she grabbed my arm. "Do they know you're hiding me?"

I told her everything, except the part about the hair ribbon on Abednego's neck. I didn't have the heart to upset her more than she already was.

Her face drooped. "Now what?"

"Sh-h, we better keep our voices down," I whispered. "I have to get you out of here—fast!"

She sulked, her hair brushing the side of her face as she leaned forward. "Where to?"

I sat on the floor, still shaking from Officer Rhodes' interrogation. "You need to do exactly what I say, no questions asked." I leaned forward, my gaze boring into hers. "No questions! It's total obedience from here on out. Just like the Amish."

Lissa's eyes almost popped. "I'll do anything to keep from going home," she said, "if that's what you mean. But what's this about the Amish?"

I felt tense as I looked into Lissa's questioning face. *This has to work*, I thought.

TEN

Downstairs, I ate Mom's delicious Hungarian goulash. And I did some fast talking to get Skip to let me stay home from the hayride.

"Pete's sake, Merry," he said. "Can't you leave your dumb cats home alone for once?"

"It's not the cats."

His fork hung in midair. "Oh, I get it. You think you might hear from Lissa again?" He paused. "Maybe you're right, Mer, maybe you should stay home."

I couldn't believe how easy that was. The second he pulled out of the driveway, I raced to the fridge, slapped leftovers onto a plate, and tossed them in the microwave. Poor Lissa. Not only was she beat up, she was probably dying of hunger, too. By the time I got upstairs with a plateful of hot goulash, she was gobbling granola like crazy.

I sashayed across the room, singing a silly song. "Are you lookin'? It's home-style cookin'!" I waved the plate in front of her nose.

"I can't wait," she said, reaching for the fork.

Just as she opened her mouth, I stopped her. "You oughta thank God first."

"But I'm starving!"

"Still, you can be thankful."

"Will you pray?" she asked.

"Sure." I took a deep breath. "Dear Lord, please bless Lissa's supper. And I need your help tonight, Lord. I know some of what I've done may not make you very happy. Especially the deceitful part. Please forgive me for that. Amen."

Lissa studied me before digging in to her supper. "It seems like you really know Jesus, Merry. The way you talk to Him, I mean."

"You can know Him that way, too," I said. "He's always there for you. Like a best friend, or . . . like a big brother. And you can always count on Him."

The tears came again and she brushed them away as she began to eat.

I hated to leave so abruptly, but time was wasting. "I have a quick errand to run now, but if you stay in my room, you'll be safe," I assured her. "I'll be back in no time."

"Where are you going?"

"If things work out, I'll tell you all about it when I get back." I felt prickles pop out on my neck.

Her eyebrows knit together into a hard frown.

"Oh, before I forget, our cleaning lady comes tomorrow," I said.

"For how long?" Lissa asked, scraping her plate clean.

"She's thorough," I said. "It'll take her till around

lunchtime. Especially when I tell her we're having company."

Lissa groaned. "Will I have to stand in your coat all day?"

"Trust me, you won't."

Lissa's shoulders straightened a bit. "Anything's better than going back home."

I grabbed my jacket and locked up the house before I left.

❧   ❧

Outside, a red moon wore a lacy cloud-shawl over its shoulders. Woodsmoke hung in the air as I hurried down SummerHill Lane. I turned off at the willow grove, making every step count. Pushing my way over the hard ground, I found the shortcut between Rachel Zooks' house and mine.

A chill wind whipped through the willows, and I pushed their swaying branches away from my face. Two crows flew high in the November sky, *caw-caw-cawing* back and forth.

Over the crest of an embankment at the edge of the willow grove, Zooks' pond sparkled in the moon-drenched light. I'd saved Levi from drowning in that pond. Hurrying, I came to a white picket fence and climbed over, then scurried across the meadow, dodging a few cow pies. I pinched my nose shut.

Like the fence, all the outer buildings on the Zooks' farm were a bright, clean white. The woodshed, the milk house—even the old outhouse. The fresh painting meant a wedding was coming.

The light up ahead in the Zooks' kitchen looked warm and inviting. At the front of the house, small kerosene lanterns twinkled in the living room. It was a large house, built by Rachel's grandfather years ago. Large enough to hold 250 or more wedding guests.

A long porch framed the front of the house. As I ran up the steps, I heard someone tooting out "Oh, Susannah" on the harmonica. Anxious to talk to Rachel, I knocked on the door.

"Wilkom, Merry," Abe Zook said as he opened the door wide. His bushy beard, beginning to gray in spots, spread from ear to ear. Tan suspenders held up his black trousers. "Look who has come," he called as Rachel came in from the kitchen to greet me. The smell of brewed coffee wafted through the house.

"Mam has shoofly pie," Rachel said, leading the way through the living room and dining room, where brightly colored china decorated the shelves.

Amish life revolved around the home and the kitchen, especially in winter. I felt the heat pouring from the large stove in the center of the kitchen. With no central heating, the stove provided enough heat for this room and the bedroom above it.

I couldn't remember visiting Rachel's family and not being offered more food than I could hold. This time was no different. An enormous pie and some sliced bologna and cheese graced the long wooden table in their spacious kitchen.

Rachel's father wandered back to his straight-backed rocking chair near the gas lamp in the corner. A German Bible, its pages brown with use, lay open on the reading table near his pie plate. But it was the pie he reached for. "*Des is gut.*" He licked his lips.

Levi and his little brother, Aaron, played marbles near the stove. Levi glanced up at me, but I quickly looked away.

Nancy, Ella Mae, and little Susie, Rachel's younger sisters, played checkers on a table in the ring of light near their father's reading lamp. Their rosy-cheeked faces shone when they looked up to greet me.

Only Curly John was missing. I didn't have to ask where he was. With just two days before his and Sarah's wedding, they were probably out under the moon, riding in his open-topped courting buggy.

Rachel's mother stopped braiding a rug to dish up a hefty serving of pie. "What do you hear from your parents?" she asked.

"They've called several times," I said, wishing they were here now. "They're excited about getting suitcases filled with Bibles into China."

She placed the pie in front of me.

"Thank you," I said, sitting at the table beside Rachel. I felt guilty being here, enjoying the peaceful Amish evening and the delicious after-dinner treats while Lissa was locked away in my room, waiting for my return.

And there was Skip. What if he decided to come home early after the hayride? I glanced at my watch, wishing I could arrange to talk with Rachel in private.

When I finished the gooey molasses pie, I wiped my sticky hands on a napkin. "Can you show me the pillow you're making for Curly John and Sarah?" I asked Rachel. It was the only way to get her alone.

"We must go upstairs a bit, Dat," she told her father as we slid out from behind the wooden table.

"Do not delay," he answered, and I knew it meant Rachel must not go off with her "English" cousin, excluding the other members of the family. Evenings were together times, and individualism was frowned upon.

Rachel carried a small kerosene lantern in one hand and held up her purple dress in the other as we climbed the stairs. I trailed close behind. When we got to the bedroom she shared with twelve-year-old Nancy, I closed the door. She placed the lantern on her antique maple dresser.

The room was scantily furnished with only a double bed, a small bedside table, and a long wooden chest— Rachel's hope chest. None of the furniture pieces matched. She opened her dresser drawer and pulled out a green-and-pink hand-stitched square pillow.

"It's beautiful," I said, admiring it closely.

"I can make one for you, Merry," she said, smiling.

"That's sweet of you, but you don't have to."

"Maybe I want to," she answered, cheerfully. "For your hope chest."

I touched the ruffled edging. "Okay," I said, ignoring the fact that I didn't even own a hope chest. Right now, I was more concerned about hiding Lissa. "I have to talk to you, Rachel. Friend to friend."

Rachel's smile faded. "What is it?"

"I need your help," I whispered. "We're having company tomorrow night and I need a place for a friend of mine to stay. Just until Thursday, after Curly John's wedding. But we must keep it a secret."

Rachel hesitated. "From Dat and Mam?"

"Yes, even from your parents." I watched her face, desperately hoping that she'd consent.

"I cannot lie about anything," she said. "I must always tell the truth."

"You won't have to lie." I felt badly about putting her in such an awkward position.

Rachel adjusted the waist of her long black apron. "I know Dat and Mam will say Merry Hanson's friend is our friend, too." She paused for a moment. "Please—I *must* tell them."

Lissa's secret was serious business. I couldn't take any chances with her safety. Rachel simply couldn't tell her parents. Not anyone! She'd have to hide Lissa, just the way I'd been hiding her.

Then it hit me—the Amish had very little contact with the outside world . . . Maybe it wasn't such a big deal for Rachel to tell her parents. I studied her, halfway holding my breath. "Okay, Rachel, you may tell them. Just so you don't spread it around."

Rachel nodded. "Jah, good. Your friend can stay in the *Grossdawdy Haus*." She was referring to the large addition to the main house, where her grandparents lived. "Grossmutter and Grossdawdy have a spare bedroom. Jah, that will be good."

"What about Curly John's wedding? Can my friend come along, too?" I asked, feeling more and more confident that I'd made the right choice.

Rachel's cheeks were pink in the dim light. "Jah, your friend must come. With you and Skip."

Just then my eyes caught the wooden clothes rack on

the wall. Rachel's clothing—for work and "for good"—was hanging there. The Amish had certain clothes they wore only for doing farm chores, and the good clothes were worn on Sundays or other dress-up occasions like weddings and singings. "My friend should come plain to the wedding," I said, overjoyed with this perfect solution to Lissa's problem.

"English don't dress plain," Rachel argued.

"This is *very* important. I promise to tell you everything later," I assured her.

Rachel and her family considered me a close friend, even though it wasn't too common for the Amish to associate closely with outsiders. Because Rachel was in her teens, the Zooks allowed their oldest daughter much more freedom, even concerning her choice of friends. Later, she would be baptized into the Amish church if she decided to follow the teachings of the *Ordnung*—the Amish blueprint for expected behavior. After that, her association with "English" friends would be more limited.

"Is there trouble, Merry?" she asked.

"No trouble." *Better not be trouble.* I remembered the way Officer Rhodes had stared at Lissa's yellow hair ribbon on Abednego's neck.

"Good, then," Rachel said.

"Is it all right if I borrow your dress for my friend?" I asked.

Rachel reached for the pastel green dress and a black apron and bonnet hanging on the wooden pegs, her eyes searching mine. "I can help you, cousin." And by the way she said it, I knew she still suspected something.

I folded the handmade garments carefully, zipping

them into my jacket for safe keeping. "When can I bring my friend to the Grossdawdy Haus?"

"The door is always unlocked. Come on over any time," she said.

"Thank you very much, Rachel," I said, relieved. "We'll probably be over first thing tomorrow."

She reached for the heavy black shawl hanging on the farthest peg. Her innocent face glowed in the lantern's golden light. "*Da Herr sei mit du*, the Lord be with you," she said, handing me the wool wrap.

❧ ❧

I chose the shortcut home. Hurrying over the picket fence, I could see wind ripples making swirls on the pond in the distance. Up ahead, the willows cast eerie shadows as I slipped through the grove. Pressing my jacket against my chest, I hurried onto the dirt lane toward my house. The Amish clothes were safe inside my jacket, and I smiled at the success of the evening.

In the distance, I heard the sound of singing. I recognized Skip's strong baritone over the other voices. Peering down the lane under the light of a winter moon, I spotted a large wagon on the crest of the hill. It was scattered with several bales of hay. Streams of light bounced around as the kids swung their flashlights.

They'd be passing my house in a few minutes. Yee-ikes! If my brother spotted me, he might get suspicious. I couldn't let that happen!

I began to run. Faster . . . faster. If I could just keep up this pace, I might make it home without being seen. My leg muscles ached. *I can't slow down*, I told myself.

Sucking in short breaths of air, I pushed forward. Harder and faster. The edge of our front yard was within reach. I forced my legs to keep moving, ignoring the throbbing pain in my thighs.

The singing was clear and strong now. My feet pounded the dirt road. No willows to hide me.

The songs grew louder as the clip-clop of horses and the rattle of the hay wagon rang in my ears. Glancing over my shoulder, I judged the distance without stopping. Then my eyes caught something across the street. Some-one—a dark, menacing shadow—crouched behind the bushes!

My heart pounded. Fear stuck in my throat. But a surge of energy propelled me across the side yard toward the gazebo behind our house. I made a dive under it, hiding there till the laughter and the songs slowly died away.

Meow!

I jumped as Abednego nuzzled my face in the dark space under the gazebo. "Oh, it's you, little boy," I said, still panting hard. I crawled out quickly and brushed the dirt off my jeans. Relieved but out of breath, I fished for my house key in my pocket.

Suddenly, I heard footsteps coming up the side yard toward me. My hand went stiff in my jeans pocket. I tried to pull the key out, but my fingers stuck clumsily in the fabric. Gasping for air, I panicked, only a few yards from the safety of my home.

ELEVEN

"Help!" I shouted.

"Mistress Merry, you'll wake the dead!"

I spun around. "Jonathan Klein, you scared me silly!" I almost hugged him, I was so relieved. "Where'd *you* come from? Why'd you hide in the bushes like that?"

He shoved his hands into the pockets of his blue winter jacket, looking confused. "Questions, questions," he said. "What are *you* doing out here?"

I ignored his question. "Are you saying you weren't hiding out front just now?"

"You know me better than that."

"But I saw someone hiding . . . I thought it was you!"

"I would never try to scare you like that, Merry. I saw you running toward your house, that's all—just jumped off to say hi."

I looked around him, worried about whoever—whatever—it was I'd seen out front. "He's probably still out there."

"Who's out *where*?"

I pulled the house key out of my pocket. "Quick, we

71

have to get inside! Someone's out front, hiding in the bushes."

"You're not making sense, Merry," he said. "I didn't see anyone."

"C'mon." I unlocked the back door. "I'll prove it to you." Without another word, I dashed to the dark living room and peered through the window curtains. I scanned the bushes with my eyes, again and again. Nothing!

"He was just there," I said, pointing.

Jon crept up behind me. "Are you sure it wasn't just moon shadows or something?"

"You don't believe me?" I shot back. "I *know* I saw someone over there."

"Sure, show me the shady, shaggy stranger," he said, starting up his alliteration routine.

"It's not funny," I retorted.

"Say that with all *f*'s."

"I'm not playing your game, Jon. I mean it."

Slowly, he turned and headed for the kitchen. I followed him and flicked on the tiny stove light. "I'm glad you're here." I felt Rachel's clothes still hidden inside my jacket.

"I can't stay," he reminded me. "I have to catch up with the hayride. The group was going to stop down the lane for a quick hike." He stopped talking and smiled like some terrific idea had just struck. "Hey, why don't you come along?"

"I would, but—" I couldn't leave Lissa with some stranger lurking around.

Jon leaned closer. "But what?" I smelled a slight hint of his peppermint gum.

"Just please stay here till Skip gets back."

"I'll have to walk all the way into town if I don't catch up with the group," he insisted, heading for the back door.

"I'll get Skip to drive you," I offered.

He suddenly seemed shy. "I shouldn't be here anyway."

"Skip'll understand when he comes home. I'll tell him what I saw."

"Really, Merry, I think you'll be fine. Just keep the doors locked." He smiled, running his long fingers though his hair. "Guess I'll see you later."

It was no use. Jonathan didn't understand. And I couldn't explain my real fear—that maybe the tall shadow out there was really Lissa's father. With a quick wave goodbye, Jon opened the back door and left.

Alone again, I groped my way through the dark hallway to the front door, shivering with fright. I didn't dare turn on the lights.

I remembered what Rachel Zook said about the Amish always keeping their doors open as I gripped the lock, double checking it. Satisfied it was secure, I peeked out once again. Maybe Jonathan was right. Maybe the moon *had* played a trick on me.

Feeling better, I headed upstairs, pulling Rachel's Amish clothes out of my jacket. I found Lissa staring at one of the pictures on my wall gallery. When I came in the room, she turned away, reacting as though she'd been caught. "I . . . uh, didn't mean to—"

"Go ahead, it's okay," I said.

She moved back to look at the photo of the flower-strewn gravestone. Leaning closer, she read the words, "'Faith Hanson, precious daughter and dear sister, in heaven with our Lord.'" Lissa stood silent for a moment. "Was your sister sick long?"

"Not long." I kept the Amish clothes hidden behind my back.

She turned away from the wall to look at me. "How'd you handle it when you knew your twin was dying?"

A lump grew in my throat, but I forced it down. "It was hard for all of us. Really hard."

"Did you cry a lot?" Her gaze penetrated me.

Uncomfortable, I looked away. "Mother cried enough for all of us," I said, avoiding the question. The truth was I'd never let myself cry about Faithie.

Lissa limped past the picture of the gravestone to more of my photography—Amish windmills, water pumps, and landscapes. There was even a picture of the playground at the Amish school, without the children. I'd always respected their wishes by not photographing the Amish, unlike some tourists who had been known to stalk young Amish children, bribing them for a snapshot.

I was relieved that Lissa didn't say anything more about crying for Faithie. Glancing out my window, I peeked through the side of the curtain. Slowly, I surveyed the area below. That's when I saw the tall gray shadow emerge from the bushes. It was a policeman, and he was motioning to someone.

Quickly, another policeman appeared, coming around the corner and across Strawberry Lane toward the house.

"Lissa!" I called.

Startled, she jerked her head. "What?"

"Quick! Kill the lights." I waved her to the window. "Two policemen!"

Terror filled her eyes as she scrambled to the lamp beside my bed. In the darkened room, we stared through the curtains, scarcely breathing.

Lissa gasped. "That's my dad! I *know* it is . . . and his partner, Officer Rhodes, he's the other one . . . the big guy."

I could hardly breathe, let alone think. "That's the cop who questioned me this afternoon," I muttered. "Why's he back?"

Then I remembered the strange way he'd looked at Lissa's yellow ribbon on Abednego's neck. What if Mr. Vyner had described what he'd last seen his daughter wearing?

Lissa grabbed my arm. "What'll we do? They're going to take me back home!"

I pulled her into the closet, the Amish clothes still draped over my arm. "I'm going to help you escape." I flicked on the light. "See this?" I held up the light green dress and long black apron. "It's your way out of here."

She reached to touch the dress, then her hand sprang back. "Ee-ew! It's disgusting."

I began to unfasten the Velcro on the front. "You'll get used to it."

She shot a weak smile through her tears. Then the doorbell rang. Lissa grabbed the dress. "I'll wear it, disgusting or not." And she began to undress.

Br-ring!

I opened the closet door to answer the phone, but

Lissa pulled me back. "You can't!"

"It could be my parents," I said. "They'll worry if no one answers."

"And it *could* be a trick." Lissa's white, fearful face said it all.

The phone rang a second time. Lissa struggled with the Velcro on the Amish dress as I counted the rings under my breath. Finally, I couldn't take it any longer. "What if Skip's calling?"

"Let it ring," Lissa insisted. She held up the black apron. "Which way does this thing go?"

"Here," I said, positioning it against her as she slipped her arms through the openings. My fingers trembled as I attached the apron with pins. "You're almost ready. I'll fix your hair." I hurried to my dresser in the darkness.

"It doesn't matter what my hair looks like," she wailed.

Back inside the closet, I parted Lissa's hair down the middle and pushed it into a quick bun, securing it with three hair clips. "Now you're plain."

The phone kept ringing.

I was dying to answer it. "How do we know it's the police?" I said. "Besides, if it's my parents, they could help us!"

Lissa's mouth pinched up like she was disgusted. "You couldn't say anything on the phone anyway. The phone lines might already be tapped."

Maybe she was right. But right or not, the ringing phone made me feel uneasy. And very homesick to talk to my parents!

Suddenly, I heard Skip's voice. "Merry! Are you home?"

I flung open the closet door and ran across the bedroom to the locked outer door. "I'm up here," I called down the steps, never so delighted to hear his voice.

"Will you *please* answer the phone?" he asked. "We've got company again."

I knew he meant he was talking to the cops. Scurrying to the hall phone, I picked it up. "Hello?"

"Oh, hello, Merry. I thought you'd never answer." It was Miss Spindler.

"Uh, we're sort of busy right now," I said. Miss Spindler's nickname was Old Hawk Eyes. She made it her duty to keep close tabs on things in the neighborhood. Seemed to me she had it down to a near science!

I could hear Officer Rhodes' voice downstairs. There was another voice, too. I clenched my teeth, remembering the voice from the phone call this afternoon. Lissa's father! He was right here—inside my house!

Old Hawk Eyes' scratchy voice continued, "I see police cars parked around the side of your house, Merry."

"You do?"

"Oh dear, it looks like—"

"What?" I interrupted. "What do you see?"

"More police," she moaned. "Oh, horse feathers! They're surrounding your house!"

"How many?"

"Well . . ." She hesitated, as though counting. "I saw at least two at your front door a while ago, but now there are two more behind your house. What in this wide world is going on?"

"Thanks for calling, Miss Spindler," I said, abruptly. "Thank you *very* much."

"But Merry—"

"I'm sorry, Miss Spindler, I have to go now." And I hung up. Thank the Lord for nosy neighbors!

There was no time to waste.

TWELVE

Downstairs, the muffled voices grew louder. Then unexpectedly, I heard my name mentioned. If a search warrant was involved, the cops would be invading the upstairs room any second!

I flew down the hall to the bedroom and tore into the closet. Cramming the black Amish bonnet down on Lissa's head, I noticed with relief that her bottom lip was nearly back to normal. "Follow me and don't make a sound," I whispered.

Lissa's lips quivered as she nodded.

"You'll need this heavy wool shawl." I snatched it up as we left the room.

"Where are you taking me?"

I pressed my finger to my lips as a wide-eyed Lissa tiptoed slowly behind me toward the back steps.

"Merry!" It was Skip again. "Get down here."

I cast a silent warning signal to Lissa as we descended the back stairs leading to the dark kitchen. With my hand gripping her tiny wrist, I peered through the window in the back door.

Two policemen were standing across the yard near the

gazebo, probably waiting in case Lissa came running out.

One glance at my friend's tear-filled eyes gave me the courage I needed. Nothing could stop us now.

"Here's what you do," I whispered. "Head for the Zooks' farm. Walk slowly—try not to limp, and no matter what, keep your bonnet on. If anyone questions you, look down, act shy." I hugged her quickly.

She clung to me. "Aren't you coming?"

"Wait for me in the willow grove. You can't miss it," I said. "You'll be well hidden there."

She clasped her hands tightly. "Merry, I'm scared to death."

"Remember what I said." I felt the tension, the stubbornness in my jaw. I was determined to take care of her. To rescue her from the abuse. If I could just get her to the safety of my Amish neighbors until my parents returned!

I took a deep breath and casually opened the back door. "See you tomorrow!" I called, pretending she was Rachel Zook.

Lissa waved back, cooperating with my little scheme.

Slowly, I closed the door, silently praying for her safety. And for forgiveness, too, from this deceitful play-acting.

I heard voices down the hall. My heart pounded as I hurried to the living room.

"What took so long, Mer?" Skip asked when I came in.

I sat beside him. "Miss Spindler's worried silly about us. She saw the squad cars. That's why she called." I looked at the policemen sitting on the love seat. *Did they buy it?*

Officer Rhodes studied me with his piercing gray eyes as if he was ready to accuse me of something truly horrible. "Heard anything more from Lissa?"

"She hasn't called here," I said, without lying.

I noticed the other policeman, Lissa's father. His face looked grim, though his lips were framed by a bushy moustache. His bloodshot eyes, small and pouched, reminded me of a sick bullfrog. I saw a ripple in his nose. How did it get busted? In a drunken brawl?

Officer Rhodes introduced him, but instead of offering to shake hands like a gentleman, Lissa's father rubbed his stubby hands together. If I hadn't known better, I'd have thought *he* was the one on trial here.

"I believe we've met," he said, nodding his froggy head. He squeezed his sausage fingers into tight fists, like he was itching to get them on his daughter. No telling what he'd do if he found her!

Officer Rhodes seemed preoccupied, brushing cat hair off the cushion. "By the way, may we see your cat again, Merry?"

Skip looked puzzled, then he chuckled. "Merry's got three cats."

Lissa's father leaned forward suddenly. "Let's have a look at them," he demanded, not in the polite way he'd spoken to me earlier on the phone.

I swallowed hard. They were on to something. Probably the yellow ribbon. Why hadn't I gotten rid of it before, when I had the chance? "I'll call the cats," I said, excusing myself.

Quickly, I ran into the kitchen. It was a good excuse to check up on Lissa's whereabouts. I hurried to the side window, so the police in the yard couldn't see. "Here, kitty, kitty," I called, pretending to search. I kept my eyes peeled for Lissa as I continued calling for the cats.

Way down the lane, I spotted a thin shadow in the moonlight, walking with a slight limp, as demurely as a real Amish girl.

Good! Lissa had made it past the cops!

Two of my cats came bounding across the kitchen floor, sliding on the rug as they came to a stop. I picked up Shadrach and Meshach and nuzzled them against my face.

Where was Abednego? And what could I dream up about that yellow ribbon without telling a lie?

My heart in my throat, I called to my wayward cat. "Abednego, where are you?" Carrying Shadrach and Meshach into the living room, I felt the hairs on the back of my neck prickle.

Officer Rhodes glared first at one cat, then the other. He frowned, obviously puzzled.

"Abednego's missing again," I explained, directing my comment to Skip.

"That cat's *always* missing," my brother said, getting up to find him.

I wished Skip would sit still. Abednego needed to stay hidden!

Staring down at the golden cats in my lap, I wondered what to do or say next. My heart throbbed.

"Abednego. Isn't that a biblical name?" said Officer Vyner, obviously trying to sound more cordial.

"Yes, sir. Abednego is the name of one of the three Hebrew children who were thrown into the king's fiery furnace."

I felt a bit hot myself.

Shadrach broke the silence by coughing up a hairball. I snickered quietly as the two cops tried to keep from grossing out.

Soon, Skip came in the room, carrying Abednego by the nape of his yellow-ribboned neck. "Here's the rascal."

"Be careful," I said, reaching out to rescue my pet.

Skip plopped him down on top of the other cats in my lap. "You've heard of three blind mice," he said, showing off for the police. "Well, here we have three dumb cats."

I wished there was a way to get rid of that yellow ribbon before . . .

Instantly, Officer Rhodes stood up. Towering over my lapful of cats, he reached down to touch Abednego.

Pph-ht! The cat hissed and sprang his claws out in defense. Officer Rhodes jumped back.

"Sorry, sir. He's real funny about strangers," I said. But the policeman approached Abednego again and the black cat leaped off my lap, scurrying out of the living room, meowing angrily.

"Why that little—" Officer Rhodes boomed.

Frightened by the thunderous remark, Shadrach and Meshach jumped off my lap, racing after big brother.

"Uh, I'll be right back," I said, joining the chase.

Skip ran after me, following a trail of cats into Dad's study.

"I'll check upstairs," I said, running for dear life up the long flight of steps. "Here, kitty, kitty." I searched everywhere. In the bathroom, even Skip's room. But Abednego had vanished. My heart pounded. I had to find him before Skip did!

Shouting and hooting came from downstairs. What was going on? I listened again. It sounded like—could it be? Were the cops actually chasing my cats around the house? It wasn't funny, but for a micro-second, I couldn't keep from smiling.

Turning back to the problem at hand, I frantically checked all of Abednego's favorite hiding places. But no cat. While in my room, I opened my dresser drawer and found my own yellow hair ribbon. I wouldn't have to lie about the ribbon—if only I could switch it with the one on Abednego's neck.

"Dear Lord," I murmured, "this is urgent stuff. I have to be the one to find Abednego. Can you please help me?" It was a desperate plea, one that needed immediate heavenly attention!

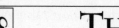 THIRTEEN

I kept searching, hoping Abednego had outsmarted the cops. Frustrated and thinking of Lissa, I sat on the edge of my bed. "Where are you, kitty?" I sang softly.

Whish, swish.

I looked down. A long black tail flicked against my ankle. Slowly kneeling beside the bed, I pulled the comforter up and peeked under. "Come here, little boy," I pleaded.

Cautiously, timidly, Abednego came.

"Good boy," I whispered, untying the hair ribbon with shaking fingers. Quickly, I replaced it with my own yellow one, an exact match, except for one thing: my initials had been cross-stitched on one end of the ribbon.

Before taking Abednego downstairs for further questioning, I tossed the old ribbon in the fruit leather shoe box in my closet. And pushed the lid down hard.

❧　　❧

"Hold him still!" Mr. Vyner commanded.

Gently, but firmly, I held my whining, hissing kitty as the fat fingers carelessly untied the yellow ribbon. I remembered the way Abednego had warmed up to Lissa. He was smart that way. He knew the difference between kind and cruel.

Roughly, Lissa's father pulled the ribbon off my cat's neck. A determined scowl swept across his froggy face. And it stayed there. "It's hers all right," he growled, handing over the evidence to his partner. "Where is she, young lady?"

I held my breath, terrified.

"Hold on a minute, Vyner." Officer Rhodes stared at the ribbon, turning it over. "These aren't Lissa's initials. Take another look."

I sighed a deep, trembly sigh, waiting . . .

Lissa's father grabbed the ribbon from Officer Rhodes, then tossed it gruffly onto the coffee table. "We're wasting our time here," he grumbled and marched out of the room.

Officer Rhodes stayed behind a few minutes, boring his stern eyes into mine. "We suspect Lissa may try to contact you again, Merry."

I could read between the lines. It wasn't so much what he said, but the way he said it.

"Yes, sir," I managed to say.

Officer Rhodes excused himself, apologizing for taking up so much of our evening. Skip got up and showed him out. When Skip got back, he collapsed in a chair. "Man, this better be the last time. I can't take all this excitement."

He couldn't? What about me!

As soon as Skip settled down in front of the TV, I hurried into the kitchen and grabbed a handful of cookies. I put them in a sandwich bag for later, still thinking about the police encounter. These guys meant business! And I knew it wouldn't be long till they were back. In the meantime, they'd probably be watching the place like hawks.

Another thought disturbed me: Mr. Vyner had seemed more angry than anxious over Lissa's disappearance! Shivers flew up and down my spine.

I waited till the squad cars left before going upstairs. Quickly, I packed my gym bag full of clothes—non-Amish ones—for Lissa. Along with the clothes, I squeezed in a few books. Some poetry, and my Bible. Then I crept downstairs, put on my jacket, and stood in the hallway hoping Skip wouldn't notice I was leaving.

Suddenly, a news announcer's voice came on the television, stopping me cold. "We interrupt our regularly scheduled programming for this bulletin: Fourteen-year-old Lissa Vyner of Lancaster county has been reported missing as of this evening," the news reporter said. "If you or anyone you know has seen or heard from Lissa, please call the number on the screen immediately. Authorities are standing by."

"Did you hear that, Mer?" Skip yelled from the living room.

I bit my lip, hoping he wouldn't wander out here. "I heard," I called back to him. "Sounds real serious."

"Yeah, you're not kidding," he hollered.

I waited a few more minutes to make sure he wasn't going to continue talking. When I felt it was safe to leave, I slipped out the back door.

Lissa was huddled against a tree deep in the willow grove when I finally got to her. She looked around as if she was still afraid of being seen out in the open. "I thought one of the cops was going to stop me at first," she whispered. "But I remembered what you said and kept my head down. I guess they thought I really was Amish."

"Wow, was that ever close!" I glanced around beneath the willow branches.

She tugged on her woolen shawl. "What happened with the cops? What did my dad say?"

"You'll never believe it." I told her everything, even about switching hair ribbons on the cat.

"You did that?" she questioned, her eyes wide.

"Lucky for us I had one the same color, but with my initials stitched on it."

"Good thinking," she said, looking positively Amish in the moonlight.

A nervous giggle burst out of me.

"What's so funny?" she asked, reaching up to touch her bonnet.

"You look like a regular Amish girl, that's all."

We approached the picket fence. "You saved my life, Merry Hanson," she said solemnly. "That's what you did."

I helped her climb over the fence in her long dress. "I did my best," I said, wishing I could say the same about Faithie. I hadn't done a thing to save her.

Lissa winced as she limped across the meadow. I reached out to steady her, thankful to have been given a second chance. This time I would not fail another human being. I would do whatever it took to protect my friend.

"Where are we going?" she asked.

I glanced at her, feeling the urgency sweep over me. Still a bit unnerved and worried about the cops showing up in the neighborhood, I summoned the courage I needed for Lissa's flight to safety. "To the Grossdawdy Haus." I pointed to the large addition on the north side of Rachel's house where her grandparents lived. "We're all set," I said as confidently as I could. "Rachel says you can stay with her grandparents till after Curly John's wedding."

"By myself?"

"Don't worry," I said, offering her a couple cookies. "You won't be alone."

We quickened our pace through the cow pasture, toward the Amish house. "I think you'll be very safe here, Lissa," I said, guiding her around through the backyard. Slowly, we approached the sun porch of the grandparents' addition to the main house. "You shouldn't have to worry about your dad or that nosy Officer Rhodes snooping around over here."

I tapped on the door.

"Hope not," Lissa said in a hushed voice.

"Wilkom, Merry," Rachel's grandfather greeted me. He smiled, nodding politely to Lissa as we walked inside.

A gas lamp hung over the kitchen table to the right of the living room. It was strange to see the house set up so much like the main house where Rachel and her large family lived. A pair of wrinkled faces smiled as I introduced Lissa to Rachel's grandparents.

"Let me show you where you will sleep." The stout

Amish grandmother wore a long gray dress with a black apron attached and a white head covering. She led the way through the living room with a large kerosene lantern just like Rachel's.

The spacious spare bedroom was sparsely furnished with a double bed, a dresser, and a cane-back chair. I noticed a small hand mirror on the dresser on top of a white crocheted doily.

"We hope you will be comfortable here," the white-haired grandmother said cheerfully. And by that I knew Rachel had filled her grandparents in on our conversation.

"Thank you," Lissa said. "Thank you *very* much!"

After the woman left, Lissa slipped off the Amish bonnet and looked around cautiously. "You're sure it's okay for me to be here?"

"Rachel said so, and she never lies." I wished I could say the same thing about myself. Up until this thing with Lissa, I'd been a totally honest person.

"They sure don't have much furniture," Lissa commented, heading for the bed with its solid maple headboard. Gingerly, she sat down.

I took off my jacket and dropped my gym bag on the floor, sitting beside her. "The Amish live super simple lives. Look at this," I said, reaching for the thick, handmade afghan at the bottom of the bed. I traced the intricate patterns as Lissa commented about the hardwood floor.

Then she spotted a paper mobile hanging in the corner. "What's that?"

"Looks like something one of the Zook kids made at

school." I got up to investigate the mobile, lifting it off its hook. "Could be Ella Mae's."

Lissa studied it, holding it close to the lantern on the dresser. "Who's Ella Mae?"

"Rachel's eight-year-old sister."

Lissa started reading the words on the mobile. "Be cooperative, be honest, be kind, be orderly." She stopped. "Yeah, I need *that* one." She pointed to the word orderly. "You should see my room sometimes."

"Believe me, I have." We chuckled in the semi-darkness.

Lissa leaned closer. "What does the rest say?"

"Be willing, be respectful," I said.

Lissa touched the mobile again. "It's something like the Girl Scouts, right?"

"Except that the Amish teach their kids to turn these words into action—it's part of growing up Amish."

Lissa was silent for a moment. The moon cast a lovely white glow over her tiny frame as she stared at the mobile. "These are hard words."

I understood what she meant. "I guess it doesn't seem quite as hard for the Amish. Maybe because their world is so different from ours. Insulated, in a way." I glanced around the room. No framed pictures of family or painted scenes graced the walls. No decorations at all. But somehow the simplicity felt calm and comforting.

I hung the mobile on its hook and returned to the window, where Lissa stood motionless. "You okay?" I put my arm around her thin shoulders.

"Look out there," she said, gazing at the large white birdhouse standing on a tall wooden pole in the yard.

"How many bird families live in there at once?"

"About twenty purple martins," I said of the four-sided birdhouse with the green gabled roof. "Martins are like the Amish—they stick together. And they return here every spring to raise a new family."

"That's what *I* need," she said softly. "A new family."

I peered sideways at her. "Maybe you're ready for God's family."

She glanced at me quickly. "How do I know God wants me in His family?"

"Because He sent Jesus to earth, that's how. And you can be adopted into the family just by asking. Then you'll have a big brother, too. One who died so you could live in heaven someday." *Where Faithie is,* I thought.

Silently, we watched wispy clouds loop over the moon like butterfly nets. I could feel Lissa's shoulders stiffen, and I knew she wasn't ready.

FOURTEEN

Lissa gripped my arm. "Stay here with me overnight. Please?"

"I would, but Skip'll freak out if he discovers I'm missing. Besides, we can't risk him getting suspicious again."

Her eyes flashed fear.

"You'll be safe with the Amish," I said, hoping I was right.

Someone knocked at the door and I went to answer it expecting to see the grandmother again.

Rachel stood in the doorway, dressed in a long white cotton nightgown and robe. Her light brown hair hung down her back in a single braid. In the golden glow of the lantern's light, she looked like an angel.

"It's good to see you again, Merry," she said, looking surprised. "Is this your friend?"

"This is Lissa," I said, purposely leaving off her last name. Just in case.

"We are ready for evening prayers." She smiled as always. Still, I could tell she was probably wondering why Lissa was dressed plain and here in their house so soon.

We followed Rachel through the kitchen, down the short hallway connecting the grandparents' side of the house to the main house. Three generations of Zooks met silently in the large kitchen, where just a few hours earlier I had snacked on shoofly pie.

Abe Zook sat in the corner of the kitchen, near the gas lamp, still dressed in his white shirt, suspenders, and black trousers. His wife, Esther, sat to his left with all the children gathered around them in a semicircle. All but Levi, who sat a short distance away from the rest.

The grandparents sat at the kitchen table across from Lissa and me, each with their own little sets of grunts and groans as they got situated.

Abe Zook picked up his German Bible and began to read, first in German, then in English, probably for Lissa's and my sake. "Romans twelve, two," he began. " 'Do not conform any longer to the pattern of this world, but be transformed by the renewing of your mind. Then you will be able to test and approve what God's will is—His good, pleasing and perfect will.' "

After a short prayer of thanksgiving for the Bible and its final authority, for the blessings which come from total obedience to its words, and for the work and toil of the day, Abe Zook said, "Amen. We'll have lights out by nine."

Lissa looked surprised. "Why so early?" she whispered as we followed the grandparents down the connecting hall to their part of the house.

"Five o'clock comes fast," I answered. "You're going to find out firsthand exactly what it's like being Amish."

"I am?" she said as we headed for her bedroom.

"Well, to start with, tomorrow's the day before Curly John's wedding. I'm sure Rachel will invite you to help with preparations for the wedding feast and all the festivities. Don't be bashful about it, okay? It's the Amish way of including you—extending their welcome."

"I can't wait to wear *real* clothes again," she said, eyeing the gym bag. "These clothes aren't my style."

I helped unfasten the waist of her long apron. Then watched as Lissa carefully folded it, placing it over the back of a wooden chair. "I can't imagine wearing a dress like this all the time," she said.

"Amish women don't seem to mind."

Lissa sat on the edge of the bed, gently rubbing her right thigh. "Guess you better get back before Skip wonders where you are," she said, looking more confident.

I nodded. "I'll see you as soon as I can after school tomorrow, okay?"

She wiggled her fingers in a tiny wave.

"Oh, you should probably wear your Amish clothes tomorrow, so you fit in around here. Just in case." I threw her a quick kiss and left.

When I arrived back home, I could hear the TV still blaring. I hurried up the back steps to my room, nearly falling over my cat trio. "Hello, little boys." Abednego followed me into my closet. "It's nice to see you hanging around here for a change."

He responded with a cheerful "Meow."

I undressed and brushed my teeth, wondering if Lissa had tucked herself in for the night. Before crawling into my own bed, I thanked the Lord for providing a safe place for her.

Slipping into bed, I thought back to my efforts to protect Lissa from her abusive father. Now that she was hidden in the Amish community, I ought to feel relieved, but a veil of guilt hung heavily around me. I tried to pray it away.

Then I reasoned with God. "I don't have a choice. I *have* to take care of Lissa. She's a helpless victim."

Exhausted, I gave up the struggle and fell into a deep sleep.

In the midst of my aimless dreaming, someone called my name. It was a familiar voice. I tried to sit up, but my head seemed too heavy to lift off the pillow.

"Merry!" A child's voice rang out.

I forced my eyes open, overwhelmed with an intense desire to see my twin again. "Faithie?" Even as I said the words, my heart beat with anticipation.

In confusion, I watched Faithie's voice take on first one shape, then another. It was as though I was observing a passage of time, from the dreadful diagnosis to the very day she died three short seasons later. Like flashing lights, the eerie forms sprang up one after another until all that was left was a frail little girl beneath hospital sheets, with sunken cheeks and lifeless eyes.

I squeezed my eyes shut, waiting, longing for tears—the tears locked away in my heart. I tried, but I could not cry, even as I saw Faithie dying before me again.

"I'm here to help you," her tiny voice called.

"Where are you, Faithie? I can't see you." I tried to shake off the sleepy haze paralyzing me. "Please let me see you again." I longed to touch her, to tell her how much I missed her. To ask her to forgive me.

A hush fell over the room. And then, I heard her voice again. *"Will you cry for me?"* The question hung like snowflakes suspended in midair, building intensity in the silence.

I struggled to speak, but the words dried up in my throat. Thrusting my hands out of the covers, I reached for her with my trembling fingertips, aching to touch her.

"Please cry for me," she said again, this time more softly.

"I want to, Faithie," I shouted. "I want to with all of my heart."

Thud!

A door slammed and I heard Skip's voice. "Merry, wake up! You're having a nightmare," he said, inches from my face as I opened my eyes.

Startled, I looked around. Disappointed.

He touched my forehead the way Mom does when she suspects a fever. "You feel hot," he said. "We better check your temperature."

"I'll be fine," I said, lying back on my pillow. "If I'm still hot in the morning, I'll check it then."

A thin golden light from the hallway allowed me to see the concern in his face. "You sure, cat breath?"

I forced a smile at his lousy nickname. "Don't worry about me."

"Okay, if you're sure." He glanced up at my wall clock. "It's almost four-thirty. Get some sleep."

I heard the click of his door as he headed back to bed. Seconds passed as I waited, listening to the deathlike silence. "Faithie?" I whispered, certain that Skip was wrong. It was *not* a dream. It couldn't be. It—she—

seemed so real! The wall clock ticked away uncaringly as I lay in bed, holding my breath for Faithie's return.

It was nearly five o'clock when I gave up trying to go back to sleep. I heard the muffled sounds of horses and buggies *clip-clopping* down SummerHill, heading for market.

Emotionally exhausted, I went to my closet, searching for one of my scrapbooks. I found it on the shelf above my hanging sweaters and shirts. Powder blue with a silver lining around the cover edges, this scrapbook held some of my best early photography.

I turned on the lamp beside my bed, propped up my pillows, and prepared for a quiet visit into the past.

FIFTEEN

Besides being a photography enthusiast, I was a scrapbook freak. I'd always been partial to pictures. For me they were better than words.

I opened to the first page. Four photos, all scenes of my childhood, greeted me. I preferred settings and things over pictures of people.

I studied the first picture—our gazebo. White and latticed, its frame was surrounded by our tall backyard maples. Flaming reds and fiery oranges told an autumn story. A sad, hopeless story—the season we were told about Faithie's cancer.

The picture had been captured by the cheap camera I'd won in first grade. Even so, the fall colors stood out as a brilliant backdrop to the stark gazebo.

I studied the second picture—a winter scene. Again, the gazebo was center stage, but it seemed nearly lost in the white fury of snow and ice. Just as our hopes had been dashed as the cancer took its toll on Faithie.

Skipping to the third picture, I remembered the spring. Mom had placed flowering plants around the gazebo, making the little outdoor room especially pretty for

Faithie's afternoon visits. The empty chaise, surrounded by spring flowers, described the emptiness I felt as my sister's illness worsened.

Then came summer. The heart-wrenching season. The fourth photo displayed a sun-drenched gazebo, minus the chaise lounge. Dad had removed it promptly when Faithie died. But along the white railing, small brown pigeons with pointed tails perched and twittered in the hot sun. Seven mourning doves—one for each year my sister had lived and laughed—had chosen to summer in our gazebo.

The mourning doves called and called during those long, scorching months. They continued for days at a time. Dad said they were calling for rain. It was bone dry, after all.

I stared at the sad scene, reliving the emotions. The mourning doves never did call down enough rain, at least not enough for the farmers around us. A fierce drought had come that year. And like the drought, my tears were dried up.

Closing the scrapbook, I placed it gently on the lamp table beside me. I turned the problem over in my mind. *How do I unlock my heart? Allow my tears to fall?*

I thought back to a long-ago morning recess when Faithie had first told me her head ached. I thought it was no big deal. She'd gone to the school nurse where she rested for a while and felt better. Several weeks later, the same thing happened. Faithie never told anyone at home and I thought nothing more of it.

When the final diagnosis came, months later, the cancer had already become too advanced for effective treatment. I blamed myself.

I closed my eyes, drifting into a troubled sleep. Morning came all too soon.

Skip knocked on my door, more calmly than usual. "Merry, how're you feeling? Still hot?"

I felt my forehead. "Can't tell," I said. But I thought of Lissa suddenly and realized how much better it might be if I stayed home from school today.

"I'll get the thermometer."

"Okay," I said, hoping for the chance to stay home. I sat up as he knocked again, feeling dizzy from lack of sleep. "Come in," I called, and the cats scampered out of the room as the door opened.

Skip came in sporting a thermometer in one hand and rubbing alcohol in the other. "Stick this under your tongue." He placed the thermometer on my lower lip and slid it into my mouth. "Now keep your lips tight." I nodded and he stepped back to survey the situation. "You look wiped out, Mer."

It turned out I didn't have a fever according to the thermometer, but Skip decided I should stay home anyway. He said I looked pale. Probably from a lousy night's sleep. Without arguing, I slid back under the covers.

"Don't forget, Mrs. Gibson comes to clean today," he said before closing the door, and without much effort, I fell back to sleep.

Around nine o'clock, I woke again. I could hear vacuuming downstairs. Feeling renewed after the extra sleep, I headed for the bathroom to shower. It didn't take long to dress and grab a bowl of cereal and some juice. I was all set to dash out the back door when Mrs. Gibson came into the kitchen. Her hair was wrapped in a blue kerchief, but her eyes were bright and alert.

Now here's a morning person, I thought.

"I hope you're feeling much better," she said. "Your brother left a note about you." I thought she was going to touch my forehead at first, but she stroked my hair instead. "If you're not planning to go back to bed, I'll clean your room now. I understand you're having company tonight."

"My aunt and uncle are coming," I said, reaching for the newspaper. I nearly choked when I saw Lissa's school picture plastered on the front page.

Br-ring! I scooted the kitchen chair back to answer the phone. "Hanson residence."

"Oh, Merry, it's you," Miss Spindler said. "I wondered who that was wandering around with Mrs. Gibson in your kitchen. Are you ill?"

"I felt a little sick this morning, so Skip said I should stay home," I explained, wondering how she could see things so far away. "I feel much better now."

"Oh, that's good." She cackled a little. "Then you'll be able to enjoy the apple pie I baked first thing this morning."

I grimaced at the thought of her coming over. I wanted to get going to see Lissa. "Uh, could you bring it over around lunchtime?" I asked.

"Well, I suppose I could do that, dear."

"Okay, thanks. I'll see you then."

"Have you heard anything more from your parents?" she persisted.

"Everything must be just fine with them, thanks," I said, eager to hang up.

"Well, that's good to know." She paused as if she was dying to discuss something else. "Merry, dear, how did everything turn out with those policemen last night?"

She would bring *that* up.

"It was, uh . . . I think everything's been cleared up." It bugged me that I couldn't articulate clearly when I felt cornered.

"That's good," she said. "And I was meaning to ask you about Rachel Zook. What's happened to her leg?"

I froze. Had Miss Spindler been watching the kitchen last night? Did she know about Lissa's Amish disguise? I cleared my throat. "Uh . . . did you say Rachel?"

"Yes, dear. I saw her limping down the lane last night after that parade of policemen arrived."

What could I say? Was Miss Spindler on to something?

She sighed into the phone. "What do you suppose Miss Rachel was doing standing out there in the willow grove all night? My, oh my, she looked cold . . . and quite alone, I must say."

Yee-ikes! I stretched the phone cord all the way across the kitchen and looked out the back door. Miss Spindler's house was about a half acre away, set on a gentle slope which made it possible to survey things quite nicely from her second floor bedroom window. And if I guessed correctly, the nosy old lady probably had some assistance— like some high-powered binoculars.

"Well, you know Rachel's at the running-around stage the Amish let their teens go through," I said, trying to steer her away from all the questions. "But I don't think you have to worry about her, Miss Spindler."

"Well, I certainly hope every little thing is just fine over there at the Zooks' house," she said. "I don't want to see fishy goings on over there."

I swallowed hard. *What did she mean?*

At that moment, I couldn't decide which was worse. Two nosy cops by night or a snoopy old neighbor by day.

In my ultra-polite voice, I said, "Thank you so much for calling, Miss Spindler. I hope you have a wonderful day and I'll look forward to that pie of yours at lunch."

"There's a dear," she said, and hung up.

In one gulp, I swallowed the rest of my juice and left the kitchen, safely out of view.

Who knows what Old Hawk Eyes would think if she saw me leave for the Zooks' farm. This was truly horrible. Here I was, stuck at home with no possible way of getting to Lissa.

SIXTEEN

I hurried upstairs to Skip's room. One of his windows faced north, overlooking the Zooks' farm. Quickly, I looked out, past the willow grove to the strip of dirt leading to Rachel's house.

More than thirty gray buggies were parked outside. The Amish farm bustled with activity as men and women hurried here and there, doing assigned chores—helping Rachel's parents prepare for their oldest son's wedding.

A group of bearded men worked an assembly line, unloading two wagons filled with wooden benches used for seating at the Sunday house services and weddings. They unfolded the bench legs before carrying them inside the house, all part of the Amish tradition.

By the looks of this large crew of helpers, the Zooks were expecting a big crowd tomorrow. I wondered what chore Rachel had invited Lissa to do.

I remembered when my first invitation had come. It was last year. Rachel and her younger sister, Nancy, had been assigned to bake molasses cookies for her cousin's wedding—three houses down the lane. It took us almost all afternoon, but when we finally finished, eleven dozen cookies graced the table. And for weeks after that, I nearly choked whenever someone so much as mentioned the word molasses.

The wedding preparations made me miss Lissa. She was probably caught up in the middle of things by now. Rachel would see to that. I just hoped that Lissa was being careful not to give herself away. It was important for her to blend into the Amish community until my dad got home tomorrow night. As for the police, they'd never think of looking for Lissa at an Amish wedding!

Dashing to my bedroom, I started pulling the sheets off my bed. In short order, Mrs. Gibson and I had the room ready for company. While she cleaned the bathroom, I sat on my bed, dreaming up a little scheme and deciding what role our housekeeper might play.

I needed a way to distract Old Hawk Eyes while I made a run for next door. *What if I got Mrs. Gibson to pay her a little visit?* I waited till she was gathering up her things and saying goodbye before I sprang it on her. "I wonder if you could do me a favor?" I said, following her to the front door.

"Of course, Merry. What is it?"

"Could you go around the corner to Miss Spindler's house and tell her everything's fine over here? She's been calling a lot lately. I think she's worried about Skip and me." I went on to tell her briefly about the visit from the police, playing it down as best I could.

"Well, of course, I'd be happy to." She tucked a loose strand of dark hair into her bandana. "Tell your mother I'll be back next week, same time. And if there's anything I can do before then, just give me a call."

"Okay, thanks," I said, waving as she headed for her car. I ran to the kitchen and hid behind the back door curtains, watching old Miss Spindler's place. In a few minutes, Mrs. Gibson's car pulled into the driveway. She got out and walked to the front door—my cue to high-tail it out of here.

Past the gazebo, down the lane, and through the shortcut I ran. By the time I leaped over the last picket fence, I was out of breath. Walking up to the back porch, I hid behind the ivy trellis, trying to see in the window. Suddenly, a familiar face greeted mine. Lissa was washing windows with Rachel!

"We could use another pair of hands," Rachel said as I entered the back door.

I sniffed a familiar scent. Glancing around the kitchen, I noticed two Amish women working over the hot cookstove, baking doughnuts and . . . molasses cookies! I tried to keep from pinching my nose shut, and held my breath instead.

"What are you doing, ditching school?" Lissa whispered, wearing one of Rachel's work dresses.

"Skip said I was too sick to go."

"You look fine to me," Rachel teased.

"I feel fine," I said, holding the bucket of water for the window washers. "Must've been that strange dream I had last night."

"A dream made you sick?" Lissa asked.

"I just got a little too hot, I guess," I said, playing it down. I backed away from the woodstove, noticing how crowded the house was with all the helpers. "Looks like everything's going well here."

Lissa nodded, looking more relaxed than she had in a long time. "Rachel showed me how to milk a cow today," she whispered. "It felt . . ." She stopped, looking up at the ceiling, then scrunched up her face. "Let's just say it was real different."

I sucked in my breath and bit my lip, worried about Lissa blowing her cover.

Rachel must've seen my concern. "Don't worry, Merry. Everything's just *plain* good."

I smiled. It was like a secret code. Her way of saying no one suspected a thing. So far.

After two more windows, we took a break. Rachel led us upstairs to her room. She showed Lissa the cross-stitched pillow she'd made for her brother's wedding gift. When Rachel's mother called, she responded quickly, leaving me alone with Lissa at last.

"How's everything going today?" I asked, eager for more details.

Lissa grinned. "You were right, I do like Rachel," she said, obviously not catching my concern. "I love it here, Merry. I really do."

I forced the air through my lips. "Please, just be careful about getting too friendly with the other young women. If you talk too much, they might suspect something. For one thing, your accent's a little off."

"Jah?" Lissa answered, smiling. "How's that?"

I motioned her away from the door. "You can't take any chances," I warned, filling her in on the phone calls from Old Hawk Eyes. "I'm worried about what Miss Spindler might do. She knows lots of Amish people around here. I mean *lots* of them."

Lissa frowned. "What do you think she'll do?"

I sighed. "Miss Spindler suspects something. I know she does. I'm just not sure how far she'll take it."

Terror returned to Lissa's face. "You mean I'm not safe here either?"

"We can't be too careful." I turned away from Lissa's piercing eyes and picked up the hand mirror on Rachel's dresser. "Have you seen yourself lately?" I held the mirror up to her.

Lissa backed away, her lips set. "Plain women never admire themselves."

I laughed. This remark, coming from her, seemed weird. "What are you talking about?"

"Their religion teaches against making an image of themselves to save or admire. It's part of not being proud," Lissa explained as though I didn't already know.

"I know all that stuff, but what do you care?"

She smiled knowingly. "I just thought if I was going to pretend to be Amish, I'd better act it."

"Well, it's a good thing *I'm* not Amish," I announced. "Life could be mighty tough without my camera."

"Maybe you could learn to make quilt designs or something else," she suggested as a tiny smile crept across her face.

I got up and went to the curtainless window. Dark Amish-green shades were rolled all the way up to allow the morning sun to heat the room. "I haven't seen Mrs. Gibson's car drive down the lane yet," I said absent-mindedly, "but I'm sure as soon as it does, Old Hawk Eyes will take up her post again."

"Well, I guess we'd better let God worry about her," Lissa said out of the blue.

"What did you say?"

Lissa ignored my question. "Did you know there's stuff about birds in the Bible?" She reached for the German Bible on the dresser. "I found a verse last night." She flipped back and forth between the pages. "I can't find it in German," she said, "but I know it's in the Bible you loaned me. Something about not one little bird will fall to the ground unless God lets it happen." A look of excitement crossed her face as she stood up, slowly making her way to the window.

I watched her stare at the birdhouse outside. There was a thoughtful, faraway look in her eyes. Lissa's voice was soft. "Birdhouses never have doors."

And without a word of explanation, I knew exactly what she was thinking.

SEVENTEEN

I hated to spoil the moment, but I wanted to impress on her one last time to be careful. "Please remember, you're being watched," I warned. "Even though Miss Spindler may have thought you were Rachel Zook last night, she *did* see the limp. The police are telling Lancaster residents to be on the lookout for certain details. Specific things."

Lissa's eyes expressed fear.

"It's everywhere, Lissa. All over the media—TV, newspapers. Like it or not, you made the front page of the morning paper today!"

"It's a good thing the Amish don't have newspapers or TVs," she said, sounding relieved. "Don't worry, Merry. I won't do anything dumb, I promise."

"We have to keep you hidden till my dad gets home. It won't be long now." I glanced at my watch. "Oh no, it's almost noon!"

Grabbing my jacket, I flung it on, muttering brainlessly to Lissa about being late for Miss Spindler's apple pie. I hurried toward Rachel's bedroom door, vowing to return later.

"Don't forget to tell Skip you're spending the night over here," Lissa reminded me.

"Good thinking." I waved goodbye.

Halfway home, I stopped walking and turned to look at the Zooks' farm through the willows. Why hadn't I told Rachel about Miss Spindler's snooping? More than anything I wanted to go back and warn her, too, just in case. But it was getting late. Old Hawk Eyes herself would be arriving at my house any minute.

Eventually, the apple pie was delivered. Miss Spindler—her hair a puff of gray-blue—brought it over. As usual, her tongue was flapping to beat the band.

"What a frightful thing it was last night. All those police officers surrounding your house!"

I tried to comfort her. "Don't worry, everything's just fine now, Miss Hawk . . . er . . . Spindler." I nearly choked! But she kept chattering on and on, never even noticing my slip up. If I hadn't known better, I would've thought she was in cahoots with the cops the way she kept talking about them.

Finally, she left, and I sat down to some lunch, topping it off with two slices of pie for dessert. Before I cut into it, I went upstairs to get my camera. I had to take a picture of the lightly browned, fork-dotted crust. I don't know why, I just did.

Click!

I ate the scrumptious dessert, enjoying the moist, delicious fruit and the crispy homemade crust. When I was finished, I aimed my camera and took another shot.

Click!

The before and after thing was something I'd picked

up at the photography contest last year. Several kids had used the approach, and when I thought about it, I realized I'd been doing it, too. Mostly since Faithie's death.

❧   ❧

Long before Skip arrived home from school, I called Chelsea Davis to get my homework assignments.

"Feeling better?" she asked.

"Lots."

"So I'll see you on the bus tomorrow?"

"Just in the morning," I explained. "My brother and I are going to an Amish wedding around noon. So I won't see you after school."

"Well, have fun with Levi," she said, chuckling. "He'll be there, right?"

"It's his brother's wedding, silly."

"Oh yeah," she said, playing dumb. "Well, maybe you'll rack up some extra credit for your social studies grade."

"Maybe. Except I'm only going to the marriage ceremony. The actual wedding sermon starts at eight o'clock and goes till about noon."

"Why so long?" she asked.

"For one thing, there are two preachers. One tells Bible stories from Creation to the Great Flood, the other preacher finishes with love stories like how Isaac married Rebecca. And, of course, there's the Amish favorite: the great love story of Ruth and Boaz."

"Ruth and who?" Chelsea asked. "I never heard of Bozo in the Bible."

I giggled. "I'll tell you about it sometime."

After we said goodbye, I headed downstairs to set the table. I wasn't sure when Aunt Teri and Uncle Pete would arrive, but I set places for them anyway.

Halfway through Skip's supper of overcooked cheese omelet, our relatives arrived. I dashed to the back door and flung it wide.

"Merry, Merry," Uncle Pete said, greeting me. He *always* said my name twice.

I hugged and kissed Aunt Teri as she followed her husband's fat stomach into our kitchen. She spied the omelet morsels left on our plates and promptly began signing to Uncle Pete. Something about stirring up a decent meal for these poor orphans, to which Skip mouthed a hearty, "Amen!"

We sat down, except Aunt Teri who moved around the kitchen with the ease of a ballerina. We were talking ninety miles an hour, probably because we hadn't seen Mom's sister or her husband since last summer. But with the talk flying so fast, we caught up quickly, especially on family matters.

The biggest news was that Aunt Teri was pregnant!

"How soon?" I asked.

Uncle Pete sat up tall and proud in his chair. "Next summer—and it's twins," he boasted, turning to sign so Aunt Teri wouldn't be excluded from the conversation.

I almost swallowed my tonsils. Thank goodness Uncle Pete started yakking his head off, otherwise it might've been obvious that I suddenly clammed up.

"Mom's gonna be so-o surprised," Skip was saying. But I tuned them out, and in a few minutes excused myself to do my homework.

As for Skip letting me sleep over at the Zooks', it was no problem. Uncle Pete, however, threw a royal fit when he heard I was going to the neighbor's so they could have my room.

"Everything's cool," I assured him. "You'll see me in time for breakfast tomorrow." No one in her right mind skipped out on Aunt Teri's mouth-watering waffles!

Skip waited to take me to Rachel's until after dessert—Miss Spindler's apple pie certainly had come in handy.

Thick clouds covered the moon as I followed my brother out to the car. The clouds were a heaven-sent blessing. Old Hawk Eyes would have a troublesome time focusing on the comings and goings of Merry Hanson on a night like this!

Skip drove me the short distance to the Zooks', even though I could've walked. Rachel and I always ran back and forth, even at night. After all, SummerHill Lane wasn't a superhighway or anything. The most traffic we ever had was the scurry of Amish buggies heading for house church or the market. I'd taken Skip up on his offer only because I didn't want to cause trouble between us. No need to stir up new suspicions about Lissa's whereabouts.

Loaded down with my overnight case in one hand and schoolbag in the other, I hopped out of the car near the wagon wheel mailbox on Zooks' private lane. I waved to Skip as he backed up and headed home. I felt good about outsmarting Old Hawk Eyes once again!

Feelings of excitement grew with each step. I thought back to my plan to disguise Lissa as an Amish girl. Sure it was risky, but it worked. Mom and Dad would be proud of how I'd handled things. Protecting Lissa from her horrible father. Sharing God's Word with her. Encouraging her . . .

Suddenly, I saw headlights coming over the crest of the hill. The car came fast, spitting dust out beneath its tires.

Was it a squad car? Had the police returned? Uneasy about what to do, I stood frozen in the middle of Zooks' private lane.

The moon slipped out behind the clouds and I could see more clearly. The car kept coming closer. . . . Anybody could see it was definitely *not* a squad car.

Concerned that the driver was out of control, I stepped back, away from the main road. The car swerved to the far left, coming straight for me. Just when I thought it would jump the ditch and ram the mailbox, the car squealed into Zooks' lane and stopped in a cloud of dust.

Instantly, I thought of Lissa's father. My mind filled in the blanks easily enough. This must be one of his wild and drunken joyrides. . . . He'd seen me walking alone at night. Yee-ikes! I was about to become a statistic!

EIGHTEEN

Just when I was close to totally freaking out, I realized the car was a snazzy red sports car—Miss Spindler's! In a split second, the dark-tinted window on the passenger's side glided down automatically.

"Hello there, Merry," she called to me, leaning over in spite of the shoulder harness. "Is every little thing all right?"

Her favorite expression, I thought, not amused by her dreadful timing. Or the way her driving had triggered my imagination.

"Thanks for asking," I said, trying not to exhibit my fright. "I'm just spending the night at Rachel's." I nodded my head in the direction of the house. "You probably heard, my aunt and uncle are staying at our house, in *my* room."

Now maybe the questions would stop. I hoped so.

She fluffed up her blue-gray kink of hair. "Oh yes . . . that's right, I do remember that dear cleaning lady of yours saying something about it." Miss Spindler stared curiously at my schoolbag, which was gaping open, revealing my camera. "It was awfully kind of her to stop by for a chat and a cup of hot coffee." Her eyes were still glued to my camera. And I could almost hear the wheels spinning in her nosy little blue-gray head.

"Well, I'll see you later." I took two steps away from her red wheels, hoping the conversation was over.

"How was the pie?" she continued.

I turned quickly. "Oh, we finished it off at supper. Thanks very much," I said, squelching the desire to ignore her.

"I'm so glad to hear it," she said and put the spiffy car in reverse, grinding the clutch as she backed down the lane behind me.

"Close call," I muttered, but I kept walking, refusing to look back. No way did I want her snooping around here with Lissa hanging out with the Zooks!

When I got to the Grossdawdy Haus, I peeked in the living room window. Lissa was sitting in one of the rocking chairs, beside Rachel's grandmother. I tapped on the door, and Grandfather Zook let me in. Quickly I explained why I'd come.

"Oh, please make yourself at home. There's always room for one more around here," the grandfather said, smiling and tapping his pipe in his hand.

Lissa seemed pleased to see me, but I knew something else was on her mind when she pulled me into her bedroom.

"Hey, you're not limping that much," I remarked as she closed the door. "It's good we got your bruises on film for my dad."

She nodded, but by the eager look in her eyes I knew the subject at hand wasn't about her recent abuse. "Remember how you told me you didn't cry when you were born?" she began. "And how I said I cry *all* the time?"

"Uh-huh." What was she getting at?

"Well, I was reading your Bible again, and I found the coolest verse." She stopped talking and I saw her eyes glisten. "Oh, Merry, I used to be so ashamed of my tears, until now."

"Show me the verse," I said, moving the lantern closer.

Placing her hand over her heart for a moment, she appeared to gather courage. Then she turned to Psalms and I peered over her shoulder as she read. " 'You have collected all my tears and preserved them in your bottle. You have recorded every one in your book.' "

Lissa looked up. "You know what that means, don't you? Our tears are precious to God—so precious He keeps them." She was obviously excited about this news.

I was silent as she took the lantern from me, placing it back on the dresser. "Thanks for bringing me to this peaceful place," she said. "I will never forget this day as long as I live."

"I'm glad you trusted me enough to help you," I said, still grasping the impact of Psalms 56:8.

We undressed for bed, and when Lissa put on a long cotton nightgown, I giggled. "You're turning into a real Amish girl, Liss."

"It's kinda fun while it lasts," she said, a sad little quiver in her voice.

"What's wrong?"

"I'm nervous about what happens next. You know, tomorrow when your dad comes home and talks to his law-yer friend."

"Don't worry, Liss. My dad'll take care of everything. You'll see."

That seemed to calm her down a bit, but it was my bedtime prayer that made a bigger difference. Before slip-ping into the creaky bed she looked at me wide-eyed. "I'm so glad you're here."

"You can count on me, Liss, you know that." I reached for my camera. "You look so cute in that Amish nightgown," I said, taking the cap off the lens. "Mind if I take a quick shot?"

She posed comically as I aimed my camera.

Click!

"Now hop in bed," I said. "And cover up with the pretty Amish quilt."

Click!

Another one of my before and after sequences was complete.

Later in the moonlight, we lay side by side in the dou-ble bed. Lissa was silent except for her breathing. Soon it became steady and slower, and I knew she was asleep. The five o'clock milking experience had taken its toll.

I, on the other hand, tossed and turned, struggling for sleep. I couldn't stop thinking about Lissa's amazing dis-covery. *God saves our tears?* Who would've thought the Bi-ble contained such a strange verse! The fact that it did had a peculiar effect on me.

At last, I slept.

❧   ❧

Long before dawn the next day, Rachel's grand-mother knocked on our bedroom door. "Rise and shine, girls," she called. "It's weddin' day!"

Lissa groaned. "I'd never make it as an Amish," she said. "Starting with this five o'clock cow-milking thing."

I crawled out of my side of the toasty-warm bed. Swinging my legs over a mountain of quilts, I tested the floor with my big toe. "Ee-e-ek!" I squealed as my bare skin touched the cold floor.

"*That's* another big problem," Lissa said, referring to the icy floor. "Hurry, let's get dressed before we change our minds!" She laughed out loud.

I noticed a tranquil look in Lissa's face. Something was different.

She avoided my eyes, looking down at the hardwood floor. "It's not polite to stare."

"I'm sorry, Liss, it's just that you seem so . . . so set-tled, so happy. It's a nice change," I said, touching her shoulder.

She went to the dresser and lit the lantern, holding it close to her face. "Is this the face of a lost soul?"

"Huh?" I frowned. *What is she doing?*

"Well, is it?" she persisted. "Look closely. What do you see?"

I inched my way across the cold floor, studying her hard.

With a confident thud, she set the lantern down on the dresser. "Remember what you said about the family of God?" She smiled. "Well, I'm a member."

"When did this happen?"

Her face shone. "In the middle of the night."

"*This* is the middle of the night," I teased.

A giggle escaped her lips. "I talked to God last night—by myself—just Him and me. I'm so-o happy, Merry, and it's all because of you." She hugged me close. "Thanks for showing me the way to my heavenly Father."

I was speechless. Life sure was full of surprises!

NINETEEN

Lissa put on one of Rachel's brown work dresses and we hurried outside to the barn. I helped by pouring fresh milk into the aluminum container and rolling it into the milk house. Tough stuff for a modern girl.

Levi offered to help on the next trip to the milk house. When I thanked him, a smile spread across his face. "Comin' to the wedding?"

I felt my face grow warm. "Skip and I'll be there."

He looked quite pleased as he straightened to his full height and marched off toward the house. I wondered what was going through his Amish head. Surely he knew better than to flirt with an "English" girl like me.

I turned my attention to Lissa, who was washing down the next cow. When she touched the cow's udder, I had to look away. Ee-ew!

Lissa got down and got dirty right along with Rachel and her brothers. It said a lot. Lissa was willing to do anything to fit in with this Amish family. Willing to do whatever she had to, to keep from going back to her dreadful family situation.

Just then Curly John ran outside looking *ferhoodled*, as

the Amish say—running around like a chicken with its head cut off—looking for his suspenders. Levi and Aaron slinked around the side of the house looking awfully guilty.

Tomorrow the real pranks would come. I'd heard of newly married Amish couples trying to do the family laundry only to discover that parts of their washing machine had been removed!

By the time we finished milking, wedding helpers, cooks and waiters, thirty in all, began arriving in horse-drawn buggies. Curly John, dressed in his new black Sunday suit, hurried to hitch Apple to the family buggy.

"He seems nervous," Rachel said as we watched. "He's off to Sarah's place, to get his bride."

I glanced at Sarah's mother, who was already checking off a long list of chores as Amish friends and relatives filed into the Zooks' farmhouse. Usually Amish weddings were held at the bride's home, but this time the groom's house was bigger, and every inch of space from living room to kitchen would be needed for the guests.

I could almost smell Aunt Teri's waffles, so I said goodbye to Rachel and Lissa. "I'll be back around noon," I said. "In time to see Curly John and Sarah become husband and wife."

We giggled. Amish or not, weddings were a blend of excitement and hope. Hope that someday each of us would be getting married, too.

Levi tipped his black felt hat flirtatiously as I left the barn. When I peered back at Lissa, I caught her eyes on us and she grinned.

All the way home, through the willow grove and down

the lane, I remembered that grin. How thankful I was for the truly peaceful way about her. Best of all, Lissa was a child of God. I could hardly wait to tell my parents. Tonight!

Aunt Teri's waffles tasted the best ever, even though I had to wash the last bites down with a glass of milk. I hurried upstairs to shower away the disgusting smell of cow manure. There were better ways to influence friends . . . and teachers.

Soon Skip was calling for me. "Hurry, Mer! You'll be late for the bus."

In a whirlwind of books and winter clothes, I managed to race downstairs, kiss my aunt and uncle, and remind Skip to pick me up by eleven-thirty. "Don't be late!" I dashed down the steps in time for the bus.

Chelsea slid over to the window when she saw me. "How ya feelin'?" She gave me a wide grin.

"Not bad for a very short night," I said, but caught myself before saying where I'd slept.

Jonathan was waiting at my locker when the bus dumped us out. "Lookin' light and lovely, Merry, mistress of mirth."

"Thanks. Feeling fine and fancy." I thought of Lissa, dressing plain, not-so-fancy these days.

"Still seeing moon shadows?" he asked.

Yeah, right, I thought. Wouldn't he be surprised to know about those moon-shadow cops?

Jon leaned his tall frame against the wall, waiting for me to collect my books. "You should've been here yesterday." His voice rose with excitement. "This place was crawling with cops—they nabbed anyone who even remotely claimed to know Lissa Vyner."

"What?" I managed to say, in spite of my cottony throat. What would he think of me, his Christian friend, hiding Lissa from the authorities?

Jon promptly repeated the whole scenario.

"Anything new on the case?" I finally asked, feeling lousy asking such a question.

"Only that they've planted informants all over Lancaster County." He shuffled his books. "Ready for class?"

I nodded, stacking up an armload of books, wondering what it would be like to have Jon carrying them. Maybe someday . . .

Halfway through history, I tuned out Mr. Wilson's droning voice. What if the cops had planted one of their nosy informants in the Amish community? Right now, someone dressed as an Amish farmer—or maybe his wife—was riding in a buggy, going to Curly John's wedding.

I sat up like I'd been hit by lightning. In the process, my notebook flew off my desk, clattering to the floor. I stretched to retrieve it, counting the minutes till the end of first hour.

Jonathan's concerned smile warmed my heart. He mouthed, "Are you all right?" from across the aisle.

I nodded, feeling foolish for reacting so strongly to my latest fears. Yet, deep in my heart, I wondered . . . Was Lissa truly safe?

TWENTY

By the time Skip and I arrived at the Zooks' farm-house, there were gray-topped carriages lined up all over the side yard. Several black, open buggies, called court-ing buggies, were parked here and there. So were a few cars and vans, belonging to non-Amish neighbors and friends.

Skip and I headed in the back way, since the service had already begun. I looked for Lissa immediately and noticed a few empty spaces on the wooden benches in the kitchen. Mostly mothers of infants, and some of the bride's aunts and cousins helping with food, sat out here. That way they wouldn't disturb the ceremony when they checked on food simmering in the summer kitchen.

Amish men always sat in one part of the house, while the women sat in the opposite end, facing each other the way they did for church. It didn't matter where "English" friends like Skip and I sat, though. We took the nearest seats available, holding the long wedding gift on our laps—a white blanket I'd found in Mom's "gift" drawer this morning. Aunt Teri had wrapped it beautifully while we were at school.

I spotted Lissa out of the corner of my eye. She was sitting near the wall, wearing Rachel's green dress and black apron. She turned slightly when she heard us come in. Wisely, she turned away.

Whew, close call! Skip would recognize her profile in a second.

Curiously, I watched as Curly John and Sarah stood before the bearded Amish bishop. Sarah looked shy and demure in her long cotton wedding dress of pale blue. Her white cape and apron matched her attendants', who sat in straight, cane-backed chairs in the front row. Curly John stood tall and proud in his black suit. I wondered if he'd found his suspenders in time for the wedding.

I leaned up a little to see him take Sarah's hand. They seemed too young for marriage, but I could see the glow of love in their eyes.

The old bishop asked Curly John a question. "Are you willing to enter wedlock together as God ordained and commanded in the beginning?"

The groom answered, "Yes."

Again, the question came. This time for Sarah, who answered, "Yes," softly.

More serious questions were asked. Then came Curly John's promises to his bride, and hers to him. At last, the bishop pronounced the couple husband and wife. Many people wiped away tears. I thought of the Lord saving our tears—the happy and sad ones. By the looks on the faces here, the tears were sober ones; the Amish understood that marriage continues until death.

No rice was thrown, no cheers were shouted, and no rings were exchanged. The mood was very serious.

My brother, however, wasn't the least bit serious. "Chow time," he whispered in my ear. And I remembered the main reason for his being here. After all, the Amish wedding feast was the most lavish part of the wedding festivities.

Complete with chicken and duck roasted in pounds of butter, and veal with rich gravy and stuffing, a kid could eat on and on into oblivion! I could almost taste the creamed celery and fresh applesauce. And washtubs full of mashed potatoes and platters piled with sausage, along with fresh bread, cheeses, and many kinds of candies. Not to mention thirty cherry pies and four hundred doughnuts!

The young people were dismissed, followed by the bridal party. The boys went outside while the girls and the bridal party went upstairs to the bedrooms, making room for dinner preparations below.

I heard the men setting up tables downstairs as I searched for Rachel and Lissa upstairs. I found them talking with the bride and groom in one of the bedrooms.

When Rachel and Lissa stepped back to let other girls visit with the bride, I went to stand beside them. "Hi, you two," I said, careful not to call too much attention to Lissa. "Everything still *plain* good?"

Rachel nodded and Lissa smiled.

I took a deep breath. "We may have a slight problem," I said, filling Rachel in on Skip being here. "He'd recognize Lissa in a flash."

"Jah, he would," Lissa said softly.

Rachel's eyes flashed concern. She probably wondered why Skip shouldn't know Lissa was here. Especially since I'd told her Lissa was *our* company! But she remained silent.

I whispered in her ear, "Remember, I promised to tell you everything?"

She nodded.

"You have my word."

Rachel brightened a bit, glancing toward the stairs. "Maybe if it works out, Skip might end up eating with some of the boys during the second shift," she said.

"No chance," I said. "He's got his mind on food and nothing this side of the Susquehanna River is gonna change that."

Rachel adjusted her apron, smiling sweetly. "I know about menfolk. Curly John and Levi are the same way."

Just then, I heard the familiar grinding of a clutch. "No, it can't be." I raced to the window. Sure enough, my suspicions were confirmed. Miss Spindler had just arrived!

Lissa frowned when she spotted her from the window. Old Hawk Eyes touched up her blue-gray puff and strutted to the back entrance.

"Was *she* invited?" I whispered to Rachel.

"All neighbors were invited for the wedding dinner," Rachel informed us. "It's *unserer weg,* our way." And I knew what she meant. The Amish were the very best when it came to making guests feel welcome—"English" or not—especially at weddings.

"What'll we do?" Lissa's eyes looked serious.

"Don't worry," I said. "I'll think of something."

It was time to go down for dinner. The bridal party had already gone. "Stay here till I can see where Miss

Spindler's going to sit," I told Lissa. I knew that Rachel would sit with her brothers and sisters near the bride and groom, so Lissa and I were on our own.

When Rachel and all the girls had filed down the long staircase, I tiptoed down partway and surveyed the situation. In a separate room, off the side of the kitchen, I saw Skip sitting with several male cousins of the groom. With that problem settled, I searched for Miss Spindler.

She was nowhere to be seen.

Quickly, I went back upstairs. Lissa was staring out the window when I found her. "Look, we're in luck. I think Miss Spindler's going to eat with the second shift," she said.

Sure enough, Old Hawk Eyes was standing out near the barn talking to a group of women. Since there wasn't enough space for everyone to sit together, the Amish had scheduled the dinner in shifts.

"C'mon, Liss, now's our chance," I said, and we hurried downstairs and found two places in the far corner of the kitchen.

When every table was full, the bishop gave the signal for silent grace. Soon, everyone was eating and talking while waiters and helpers scurried around like worker bees, serving tables. Lissa seemed perfectly relaxed with the set-up, in spite of possible threats to her security lurking outside . . . and in the next room.

I constantly checked the window, hoping Miss Spindler would stay put at least till we finished eating.

After the final dessert came another silent prayer. Then the first shift of guests were to leave the house and go outside while the next group came in. Nervously, I steered Lissa away from the kitchen door, walking in front of her all the way to the front door, trying to avoid a direct encounter with Skip.

Once outside, the first shift of guests went around inspecting the farm. Abe Zook passed out candy bars, visiting and joking with old friends and neighbors. Fortunately, it was a mild day for November—cloudy, but mild—so a light jacket was all I needed. Lissa wore a wool shawl like the other women.

We tried to stay in the middle of the group of guests touring the farm, dodging Skip by hiding behind the barn door once. Later, we maneuvered our way past him again by climbing the ladder to the hayloft.

"I'm gonna schedule a nervous breakdown when this is over," I said, falling back into the hay.

Lissa tucked her Amish dress under her legs and pulled her shawl close as the dust settled. "What a day. I'm too stuffed to be scared!" She rubbed her stomach. "Have you ever seen so much food in your life?"

I groaned, holding my middle as I sat up in the soft hay. As I did, I spied Miss Spindler standing in line to go into the house. She happened to glance our way through the open barn door. I felt uneasy staring back at her, but then, unexpectedly, she pulled something out of her purse. Binoculars!

"Duck down," I whispered.

Lissa obeyed.

I sat there, straight as the barn rafters above us, as Old Hawk Eyes gawked at me through her powerful glasses. "She's up to no good," I said like a ventriloquist through a fakey smile.

"What's she doing now?" Lissa asked from her bed of hay.

I watched as the old woman stuffed the binoculars into her purse and marched off to her car. "I think we're set. Looks like she's leaving!"

"Really?" Lissa sat up like she'd popped out of a cannon.

I pushed her back down. "Not so fast."

But it was too late. Old Hawk Eyes had glanced back just then and spotted her. Opening her car door, the old sneak leaned down, casting a leery look back at us. *Now* what was she doing?

I zeroed in on her hands, clocking her every move. That's when I saw the cellular phone. "Oh no! This is so-o bad!" I wailed.

Lissa sat up again. "What is?"

"We're toast—we're finished!" I groaned.

Old Hawk Eyes peered over her shoulder as she talked on her phone.

"She must be an informant," I cried, watching her in disbelief as she pointed triumphantly at the barn—at us!

"How do you know?" Lissa asked.

"Can't you see—she's calling the cops!"

TWENTY-ONE

I grabbed Lissa's arm, pulling her out of Miss Spindler's line of vision. "C'mon, let's make a run for it. We still have time!"

Lissa's arm stiffened. "Wait!"

"There's no time to wait. Let's go to the Grossdawdy Haus. I'll hide you there!"

"No," Lissa shouted.

I whirled around, staring at her incredulously. "What did you say?"

"I can't keep running, Merry. It's time to tell the truth." Her face had a look of peaceful determination. I wanted to throw my arms around her, to take care of her, to talk sense to her. But her words rang out, "I'm going to do the right thing. When the cops come, I wanna tell them about my dad. I have the courage to do it now." She put her hand on her heart as she spoke. "And," she added softly, "we have proof—remember the pictures you took?"

"Are you sure about this?" Something in me still wanted to keep her from going through with it.

"It's the right thing," Lissa insisted, studying me. "I

can almost tell what you're thinking, Merry, but please stop worrying. I'll be fine. I'm a *member* now." Her face lit up with a rainbow smile.

Police sirens began to squeal, soft at first, then louder as they sped their way up SummerHill Lane.

Lissa's tears threatened to spill at any moment. "You're a good friend," she said. "You're my sister, too, don't forget. We're part of the same family now."

I hugged her close. "I want you to be safe, Lissa. Forever and always."

The slamming of squad car doors and the thud of footsteps signaled the end of our time together. A crowd of bearded men gathered near the barn. Their Amish wives and children scurried to the safety of the house.

Miss Spindler's scratchy voice could be heard over the chatter of German as Amish husbands and fathers hurried to form a human barrier around the barn. The Amish were peace-loving people who would not allow outsiders to take away one of their own, especially an innocent young girl like Lissa.

"In the hayloft!" Miss Spindler shouted.

I watched as Officer Rhodes and several other policemen approached Abe Zook and two Amish bishops. They showed their badges, but Abe shook his head slowly, standing his ground as he blocked the open barn door with the others. The police persisted, and I strained to hear, but they kept their voices low and calm, trying to strike a bargain, no doubt.

I turned to my friend. "Quick! Take off your bonnet," I said. "Show them your short hair! The Amish will know you aren't one of them."

Lissa followed my suggestion and removed her bonnet. Her shoulder-length hair fell around her neck. Gasps and shouts rose up from the crowd, and Officer Rhodes moved through the barricade as the Amish parted, astonished.

Before Lissa left the hayloft, I took her hand in both of mine. "You okay?"

She nodded. "What about you?" Her blue eyes cut to the quick of me. "Remember your tears, Merry. They're precious to God." And with that, she scooted through the hay toward the loft ladder.

"I'm praying for you," I whispered.

Officer Rhodes, his piercing eyes and that businesslike chin, waited for Lissa to climb down the ladder. Just as she reached the bottom, a woman came running through the crowd—Lissa's mother! Her cries of joy rang out as she held out her arms to her daughter.

❧   ❧

I stayed in the hayloft long after things settled down. Lissa told her story—all of it—to the police. Her mother seemed eager to verify the occasions of abuse. She even said that Lissa's running away had had its merits. It had startled her into taking a hard look at the abuse she and her daughter had suffered. Four days without Lissa had given her the strength to arrange a confrontation with her husband. Best of all, Mr. Vyner had consented to treatment and extensive counseling. It was safe for Lissa to go home!

Lissa and her mother walked arm in arm to a waiting squad car. The line of police cars stirred up a trail of dust on Zooks' lane as they made their way to the main road. The Amish men milled around, whispering and shaking their heads.

I knelt in the hayloft, watching till the last car turned onto SummerHill. Lissa's words echoed in my brain. *"Remember your tears. They're precious to God."*

I scurried down the ladder to the Grossdawdy Haus. It was time for a date with my camera. An overwhelming desire spurred me on as I hurried to the room where Lissa and I had slept. Locating my camera, I ran out the back door. A lump caught in my throat as I passed the martin birdhouse in the side yard. I paused to look up at its many-sided refuge. *"Not one little bird will fall to the ground unless God lets it happen,"* Lissa had said.

I swallowed hard, and for the first time in a long time felt the sting of tears. Heading for the main road, I held the tears in check until I could be alone with them. And with Faithie.

At last, I stumbled into the small cemetery where my twin sister was buried. The gentle hills surrounding the white gravestones had been alive with wild flowers six summers before. There, I'd placed yellow daisies on her grave under a peaceful sky, setting up the shot for that long-ago special picture.

Now as I stood here, camera in hand, it was as though I'd never cried in my life. My soul was bursting, needing an outlet—wanting to make up for all the years of pain. The pain of blaming myself for Faithie's death.

I knelt in front of her gravestone, leaning my head on my arm as I sobbed. "I miss you, Faithie. I miss you . . . with all my heart."

The tears, locked away for so long, began to cleanse me. I cried the pain away, forgiving myself for the years of false blame, while a November wind wrapped its gentle whispers around me.

I don't know how long I knelt there, but slowly I began to pray. "Thank you, Lord, for loving me enough to care about the tears I cry." I wiped my cheeks. "And thanks for Lissa . . . for helping her show me the way to peace."

Looking down, I noticed a clear puddle on the ledge of my sister's gravestone. My tears. Thoughtfully, I reached for my camera, adjusting it for shadows and dim light. Then, carefully I aimed, creating a focal point: my fallen tears, with Faithie's gravestone as a backdrop.

Click! My before and after gallery was complete.

The sun poured through the clouds, creating a brilliant light. I squinted into its brightness, slipping the camera over my shoulder, and headed for home.

FROM BEVERLY ... TO YOU

❧   ❧

I'm delighted that you're reading SUMMERHILL SECRETS. Merry Hanson is such a fascinating character—I can't begin to count the times I laughed while writing her humorous scenes. And I must admit, I always cry with her.

Not so long ago, I was Merry's age, growing up in Lancaster County, the home of the Pennsylvania Dutch—my birthplace. My grandma Buchwalter was Mennonite, as were many of my mother's aunts, uncles, and cousins. Some of my school friends were also Mennonite, so my interest and appreciation for the "plain" folk began early.

It is they, the Mennonite and Amish people—farmers, carpenters, blacksmiths, shopkeepers, quiltmakers, teachers, schoolchildren, and bed and breakfast owners—who best assisted me with the research for this series. Even though I have kept their identity private, I am thankful for these wonderfully honest and helpful friends.

If you want to learn more about Rachel Zook and her people, ask for my Amish bibliography when you write. I'll send you the book list along with my latest newsletter. Please include a *self-addressed, stamped envelope* for all correspondence. Thanks!

Beverly Lewis
%Bethany House Publishers
11300 Hampshire Ave. S.
Minneapolis, MN 55438